Ava was going to tear him down, touch by touch, rid him of any further resistance

Slowly her fingers slid down his taut chest, venturing lower still, and Justin continued to keep his hands fisted at his sides. "You know all about bombs and weapons, but do you know what to do with me?" she asked.

"I know exactly what to do with you, Ava. You just trust me on that."

Nothing mattered but the way Justin watched her—alert, completely attentive, his brown eyes fixed on hers even as he struggled to remain unaffected.

Hard to do when he was completely naked. She figured it was time to even the playing field.

One small step back and her shirt floated to the floor with a soft *woosh*. The cool air hit her skin and her nipples tightened as he sucked in a breath and just stared. "You say you know what to do with me, Justin—now prove it."

Blaze™

Dear Reader,

I've always been fascinated by reunion stories. Hearing about people who have been separated from their first loves for years—and sometimes for decades or more—and end up finding their way back to one another is what inspired this story.

Beyond His Control is about Justin and Ava, who are both, for all intents and purposes, still deeply in love when the book begins, despite years of being apart. Ultimately, they learn that they have to get beyond their past to clear the way for their future. So mix that romantic tension with a little suspense and intrigue, and the reunion between the Navy SEAL and the assistant district attorney will be something neither one is prepared for...but is unable to resist.

Enjoy!

Stephanie

P.S. I love hearing from readers! Please come on over and visit me at www.stephanietyler.com.

STEPHANIE TYLER
Beyond His Control

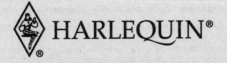

TORONTO • NEW YORK • LONDON
AMSTERDAM • PARIS • SYDNEY • HAMBURG
STOCKHOLM • ATHENS • TOKYO • MILAN • MADRID
PRAGUE • WARSAW • BUDAPEST • AUCKLAND

ISBN-13: 978-0-373-79388-4
ISBN-10:   0-373-79388-X

BEYOND HIS CONTROL

ABOUT THE AUTHOR

Stephanie Tyler writes what she loves to read—
romance with military heroes and happy endings.
She has long since stopped trying to control
her characters, especially the Navy SEAL alpha
males that she's thrilled to be doing for Harlequin
Blaze. She lives in New York with her husband
and daughter. You can find out more about her by
visiting her Web site, www.stephanietyler.com.

Books by Stephanie Tyler

HARLEQUIN BLAZE
315—COMING UNDONE
327—RISKING IT ALL

Don't miss any of our special offers. Write to us at the
following address for information on our newest releases.

Harlequin Reader Service
U.S.: 3010 Walden Ave., P.O. Box 1325, Buffalo, NY 14269
Canadian: P.O. Box 609, Fort Erie, Ont. L2A 5X3

For Mom and Dad, for always being there
and for always believing.

1

THIS WAS THE PERFECT mission—unbeatable, the kind Navy SEALs like Justin Brandt dreamed about, prayed for and rarely got.

His target was locked in. No opposition in his periphery. He maneuvered through the water easily, focused on his one, his only intent. The temperature had to be close to eighty degrees and the sun was starting to go down. Darkness gave him the perfect cover, especially with the moonlight reflecting dimly on the water.

There would be no stopping him.

He closed in, swift, silent, his one-hundred-pound advantage on the intended target rendering resistance futile. He met his prey with determined contact. There was a slight struggle, some splashing, and then, success, at last.

"Justin, I have to check on dinner." Monique giggled as she held the bikini top he'd just unhooked against her breasts in one last attempt to subvert his efforts.

He held her, her back pressed against his chest, with no intention of letting her go. "Not hungry. Check on me instead."

He nuzzled her neck as he eased the tiny squares of fabric away from her. She gave up protesting and the garment in question floated away. He turned her to face him, and when she smiled up at him, he prepared to sink his body into her eager one. Because this was what he needed. Twenty-four hours in her arms, skin on skin, and he'd be a new man.

Or at least that's what he told himself now. He'd have his regrets later, but he was in the moment and that's what mattered.

She moved her mouth closer to his ear, and he waited to hear her tell him she wanted him, that she couldn't hold on anymore, because he was going to take her so well the entire neighborhood was going to know about it... "Justin, your clothes are ringing."

"I'm not wearing any clothes, so ignore it." He took her hand, guided it between his legs.

"Sounds like it might be important," she said, glancing toward the jeans he'd pulled off hurriedly and left in a pile on a lounge chair where his cell and beeper had started to ring angrily in tandem. Never a good sign.

"Damn," he muttered. "Don't move." He pulled himself out of the pool and rifled through his jeans.

"I'll be right back," Monique said. She'd followed him out and headed inside, her bikini top left floating in the water. He stared after her, and then flipped the cell phone open with a groan.

"This had better be world war frigging three," he said by way of hello. A low chuckle answered him, and immediately his focus shifted. It was Turk, aka Leo Turkowski—his best friend from childhood, and this sure as hell wasn't a social call.

"Close enough, buddy." Turk was smoking again. Justin could hear him take a deep drag and exhale. Normally, he would have called his friend on it, since he'd promised everyone for the millionth time he'd quit for good, but it wasn't the time for a lecture. "You busy?"

Monique chose to come back out of the house at that moment, the lights from the kitchen highlighting the fact that her bikini bottoms were now conspicuously absent. She handed him a beer and trailed a finger along his neck before slipping back into the pool. He fought another groan and put the beer down. "What did you do now?"

"What did I interrupt?"

"Nothing. Really," Justin lied through clenched teeth. It had been a long, dry deployment for his entire team, who were stationed in Virginia. Every eighteen months they deployed. This time, their six-month stint had found them in the mountains of Afghanistan working recon missions—his specialty. The team had taken some heat, taken down some tangos and returned slightly worse for wear and ready for some downtime.

He'd been home for less than twelve hours before he hit a local bar and met up with Monique, a full-time stewardess, part-time actress whose schedule seemed as busy as his and who'd told him back at the bar that she didn't want any strings. It was goddamned perfect.

But when a friend called, his one-night stand would be shoved to the side no matter how much it hurt. What doesn't kill you makes you stronger and all that crap.

He heard the scratch of a match and a deep inhale as Turk lit another cigarette. "You on leave?"

"Four days' worth."

"I need some help," Turk said quickly, like it wasn't easy to ask.

"Name it."

"It's about Ava," his friend said quietly, and Justin's stomach dropped at the mention of Turk's younger sister. Ever since Turk started working deep-undercover cases for the DEA, he'd asked Justin to be on call to help Ava. Turk and Ava's father had died when Ava was still in high school and they had no significant family, save for each other.

Justin had agreed, of course, but in all the years Ava had his phone number she'd never, ever used it. To be fair, he hadn't used hers either. "Is she all right?"

"She bit off more than she can chew. And this time, it's going to bite back."

"Start talking, man. I need more information." Justin was already pulling on his jeans, not giving a damn about being soaking wet.

"I can't give you much. Just go to her."

This was nothing Justin hadn't done before. He'd always managed to do so without Ava knowing. As if guarding her from afar could make up for the way he'd hurt her. For the way he'd hurt them both.

Secrecy was better for all of them. And he'd always been able to take care of the problems plaguing her without much effort—usually some lowlife threatening her because of her job as an assistant district attorney, and because of her tendency to refuse to stand down when she was up against it.

It was a trait that ran long and hard in that family. And while Justin himself had a healthy appetite for living right out there on the edge, Turk and Ava brought it to an almost artistic level without even trying.

But this time, something in the tone of Turk's voice didn't sit right with Justin. "Tell me more."

"This is just between us, Justin. There's a possibility that her new case could blow my cover," he murmured, and Justin knew what his friend said could mean a death sentence for him, no matter the case Turk was on. It also meant that Justin couldn't bring in the local authorities for backup. "She's involved in something big and she doesn't realize it. You need to get to her tonight and get her out of New York."

"Where do you want me to take her? Maybe she needs more protection than I can give her."

"You're the only one I can trust with this right now." Turk paused for a long second, as if he wanted to say more but couldn't. "It's not going to be easy this time, Justin."

"Dammit, Turk—don't do this—" But the phone clicked on the other end before he could finish. Frustrated, he slammed it against the table and stared up at the sky for a few minutes.

Turk had joined the DEA around the time Justin made it through BUD/S training and moved into SQT, the final step before he received his Trident. He and Turk were always helping each other out, especially when one of them found himself balls deep in something, but Justin had never heard fear in his friend's voice when Turk called for a favor. Not like this.

Turk was so deep undercover that he couldn't get out in order to protect Ava.

But protect her from what?

Justin closed his eyes, thought about what would've happened if he hadn't been home now—if he'd still been deployed and God almighty, his instincts were screaming.

If he hauled ass, he could get to Ava before midnight, maybe hitch a ride on a helo from Virginia to a base in New York. Then he could rent a car and drive to Westchester County. And that would've made him happy if the thought didn't cut him right off at the knees.

Nine years had passed since he'd actually had more than peripheral contact with her. Years full of some of the worst memories of his life, some of them softened by time and by a job he excelled at. A job that kept him too busy for more than a passing fling and no more commitment than a few hours could bring.

At one time, Ava had promised she'd be there for him. No matter what. That she trusted him. And then she'd never given him the chance to explain—the day he got married she skipped town and never looked back.

You wouldn't have been able to tell her anyway.

Yeah, loyal to the end. Loyal and stupid. And young—too young to know any better, although it only made him feel marginally better to be able to blame his stupidity on youth and misguided loyalty.

It's not going to be easy this time, Justin.

With Ava, it never was.

"YOUR HONOR, Miss Turkowski is making a mockery of this case, and her antics are becoming a hindrance to the prosecution." The defense attorney clenched his fists and made a face Ava recognized immediately as exasperation. The judge wore it, too, as did pretty much any man Ava had ever known.

"Your Honor, a continuance is not on the people's short-list of wants. However, some new evidence has come to my attention that will showcase the defense's arguments in a whole new light," Ava said.

Before anyone could protest, she turned to Paul, her new assistant on the case, and in a perfectly choreographed move, he handed her the file folder she needed to present to the judge. She bypassed the defense council, a man she'd often gone up against and with whom she had a fifty-fifty loss/win split and handed the folder off.

She loved this moment—when she commanded the attention of every single person in the courtroom. She loved it because it didn't happen quite as often as she would've liked, and when it did, she savored it more than dark chocolate and good sex, neither of which she'd had time for lately.

But this was certainly not the moment to muse about that. Not when she was about to win this case.

The judge peered at her over the top of his glasses. "A.D.A. Turkowski, how did you come upon this information?"

"My source is protected, Your Honor. But, as you can see, the evidence has been verified by forensics."

"So it has." The judge closed the folder and handed it off to the defense. "You might want to take a look at this before you make any more motions on behalf of your client."

They were talking plea in less than two minutes, in hushed tones up by the judge, and Ava and the defense attorney agreed on a plea and punishment that would be put into place as soon as his client agreed.

"I wish all my cases wrapped this quickly," Judge Barrett told them.

"I don't," defense council mumbled before walking back to his client. Ava headed to her side of the courtroom, the smell of victory mixed in with the usual smell of the courtroom—a combination of stale air, fear and old coffee.

Paul was busy putting his files in order. He looked harried, a perpetual state of affairs for any new lawyer working in the D.A.'s office, and one that never got any better. She'd just learned to hide it well.

"Nice job," Paul said. "Stanton's not happy with you at all."

"Stanton can kiss my you-know-what."

"From the way he looks at you, I think that's what he wants."

"Well, he's not getting it," she said. She certainly wasn't going to whine about her attractiveness. In her opinion, she'd had nothing to do with it. It was all good genes and such, and she knew the difference between using her mind and using her body to get what she wanted. She also knew how to use both simultaneously, but most men didn't seem to enjoy that.

She sighed, realized her feet were killing her. The price of trying to have fashionable feet to offset the conservative, mostly black attire she wore when she was on the job. She sat, kicked off a shoe and bent to massage a cramp in her arch.

"I'm late for a deposition. Are you going to need me tonight?" Paul asked.

She needed something tonight, but work wasn't it. "No, no, take the night off. You deserve it," she said, mainly because Paul looked more stressed than he usually did. "Is something wrong?"

"It's this case I've got." He looked pained as he went into the details. "It's a domestic abuse case…"

"And the victim's decided she doesn't want to testify."

"It's an open-and-shut case, Ava. She could get him out of her life for good and she won't."

"Don't be so hard on yourself, or on the victim," Ava said, not wanting to break it to him that he'd have much tougher cases soon enough, ones that would wrench his heart out.

She'd been there, more than once, but especially with the Crafton case. She would never forget that one, or the look on her client's face when Ava had been forced to admit that the man who'd raped Martha Crafton and killed Martha's husband wasn't going to jail at all, was actually going free because the D.A. had bigger deals to turn in exchange for the murderer's testimony.

Thinking about that horrible day when her boss told her to cut the guy a deal made her stomach clench. In Martha's eyes, no matter how many other cases Ava tried and won, no matter how many other men and women she sent to jail, she'd always be a failure.

She'd been told many times that her job would eat her alive if she let it, if she didn't learn to shake it off, let things roll off her back. She had a lifetime of habits to unlearn, and so far, her success rate in that department was *not* looking good.

"Just keep moving forward. It's all you can do," she said. "Now get out of here before you're late."

"Thanks, Ava." Paul pushed his way out of the courtroom to head across town and she shouldered her briefcase and pushed through the mob of people as well. Not bothering with the elevator, she took the stairs down, went out the back entrance and debated going back to the office for only a second before getting into her car and heading for the freeway instead.

She really wanted to be home at a decent hour tonight. She deserved it. Although she knew she'd be working once she arrived home—she'd been handed a new case last week. It was another seemingly cut-and-dried domestic abuse case, but as Paul now seemed to understand, there was nothing cut-and-dried about these cases.

Every case she won was not only a personal and professional victory, it was building her a stellar reputation as a strong women's rights advocate.

She wasn't always successful, not nearly as often as her pride would've liked, but her track record put her at the top of the A.D.A. list. She was being fast-tracked—to what, she wasn't sure, but she'd heard the whispered rumors about herself too often to ignore it. Not that any of the rumors mattered. Justice was what mattered, a sense born and bred into her thanks to her father and his career, first with the army and then the DEA. He'd always been fighting the bad guys— and she always did her best to do the same.

The fact that a majority of her cases were garnering her more of the spotlight meant she'd also received her share of threats from the men she prosecuted and their families. That part was only going to get worse, her boss had warned her, but she'd grown up surrounded by men, was able to put up her own version of male bravado when she needed to. She'd learned to shoot and carried a gun wherever she went, learned self-defense moves and knew to watch her back.

She'd also learned that being on guard all the time was exhausting.

Now she guided her car, weaving through the typical New York City traffic heading east on the Henry Hudson. She thought of her little slice of land—and the small Cape Cod–style house she called home. She lived an hour outside of Manhattan in the hamlet of Carmel, and by the time she'd pulled into the driveway, the ride home with the top down and the radio blasting had relaxed her.

Still, she looked over her shoulder before going into the house and wished for the thousandth time she'd thought about buying a house with an attached garage.

Her older brother, Leo, had reminded her of that after the fact. She dropped her stuff, kicked off her shoes and began stripping off her business attire on the way to her bedroom. In fact, she hadn't heard from Leo in three months. It was driving her crazy, even though he'd warned her ahead of time that it would be this way on most of his assignments.

The only person who might have heard from Leo recently would have been Justin. He was her brother's best friend and still referred to Leo as Turk—his high-school nickname. At one time, she'd called Justin her best friend, as well.

Call Justin if you have any problems, Leo had repeated the last time she'd seen him, slipped her a piece of paper with a phone number on it the way he always did before he left on assignment. That paper was sitting in the bottom of her fire-safe with her other important documents, but she'd memorized that number. Thought about using it every single day for the past three months even though there had been no trouble in sight. At least nothing out of the ordinary.

Leo knew she wouldn't call Justin unless there was a major emergency, but she also understood why he kept giving her the number. Justin was the closest thing to family she and Leo had since their father had died when she was seventeen.

Ava had grown up running wild. Her mom left when Ava had been just thirteen, and in need of a mother the most.

She'd had to turn to her father and Leo for dating advice instead of her mom—both their mantra being, *you're not dating until you're thirty*, so no, that hadn't worked out well after all.

For the next few years, until they moved from North Carolina to Virginia, she'd taken on a lot of the household responsibilities. Her father was away too much to do so and Leo had no interest in things like grocery shopping or cooking.

She'd also found time to maintain a straight-A average—with a slight bit of coercion, first from Leo and later, from Justin, and have a normal social life. She didn't want anything further to disrupt their family, and she knew enough to know that social workers would have a field day if they knew her father was sometimes away for a month at a time.

Still, something inside always pressed her to go further and further to the edge, test the limits. It was a need she couldn't really control, something bred into her from her father's genes, she supposed.

Her father had been in the army—Delta Force, then moved over to the DEA at the request of her mother, who'd somehow thought that a government agency would be a safer bet. She figured she'd have her husband home more and not taking off at a moment's notice.

But her mother had been wrong because her father could find trouble just as efficiently and effectively as Ava and Leo could.

Which, of course, explained Ava's want of Justin. At the time, Justin *had* been trouble—the supposed black sheep of his family and honestly more interested in keeping her out of trouble than finding it himself. Her best friend.

She'd thought for sure they had a future together, was still haunted by that one night when she'd finally gotten through to him—or so she'd thought, the one time she'd been able to have him stop seeing her as his closest friend's little sister and he'd actually touched her…

The best and worst night of her young life. The night Justin kissed her…almost made love to her.

The day before he'd announced to her that he was marrying someone else, a girl Ava hadn't even known he was dating. A girl he'd gotten pregnant.

Nine years had passed faster than she could've imagined then, when she was just seventeen and crying so hard over Justin's betrayal she could barely breathe. Still heavily in grief over her father's death, she'd thrown herself into academics. When Leo announced he'd been accepted into the DEA, it made her turn away from him and refocus on her own career. Something that was all hers, which no one else could ever take away.

She told herself she'd been lucky that nothing had ever worked out with Justin. Where would she have been today? Worrying constantly about his safety? About when he'd return? If he'd return? Even though she'd been taught at an early age that you never, ever used the word *if* in conjunction with a military deployment. No need to tempt the fates.

Not that she didn't worry about him and Leo in secret, all the time, anyway.

There had been men during the years since she'd seen Justin. Too many, probably, in some kind of strange attempt to exorcize him from her mind and her dreams. But between her job and her lack of interest in any of these guys, because she'd always been too guarded for her own good, she'd never had much more than casual relationships. Even her most recent romance, which had lasted six months, ended because it had gotten too serious for her. Instead, she put in late nights at the office and fielded hate mail and death threats and worked hard to put the bad guys in jail and tried her best not to let the past overwhelm her.

You never even called Justin about his baby or the divorce.

She'd been too hurt to even think about Justin's loss. It had been wrong, selfish and, in her eyes, unforgivable enough that she'd never been able to contact him before this. And the worst part was that she knew that Justin, probably more than anyone else, understood why, and not just for the obvious reasons.

She'd heard, through the good old grapevine, that Justin's ex-wife had remarried, had more babies, and that Justin hadn't gotten involved with anyone significant.

She wondered if he'd been keeping tabs on her, too.

She reached for the phone, wondering if this time she'd actually go through with it. But the phone rang as her hand touched the receiver, and jolted her firmly back to reality.

She didn't know the number on her caller ID, and answered with a wary hello.

"I've got a lead for you on the Mercer case." She recognized the deep garbled voice of an informant she'd gotten solid evidence from several times in the past, thanks to some of her connections with the New York City Police Department.

Most informants couldn't be trusted any farther than she could throw them, but she didn't have much choice. "I'm waiting," she said.

"Not over the phone. In person. At Grandpa's Bar. Midnight." He hung up before she had a chance to respond. Didn't matter—she'd be there.

She had to find out what everyone else knew about Susie's disappearance.

2

AT A TABLE in the back of the dim bar, the man Ava knew only as Sammy downed the third beer she'd bought for him. Ava, in turn, played with the label on her first and only bottle and tried to appear patient.

Sammy was a good-looking, fast-talking con man whose penchant for gambling had gotten him into some bad situations. But his time spent around other recently paroled convicts afforded Ava, and the officers she often worked with, insight into cases they might never have broken otherwise.

Finally, Sammy spoke. "They got me again. I'm going to need your help."

She sighed, knowing the "they" referred to his parole officer, and the help, no doubt, involved a gambling scheme gone bad. "I thought you were getting out of the game."

"It was a setup," he protested.

"I'll talk to your parole officer but I can't promise anything, Sammy. You might be looking at some jail time."

Sammy nodded, because he knew. Still, he'd give her information in an attempt to reduce his sentence. "I hear you're looking for that Susie Mercer woman."

Keep it cool, Ava. He really doesn't know anything. "Have you heard where she is?" she asked, and Sammy shook his head roughly.

"No. I don't know where she is, but I know *who* she is." His voice was so low she could barely hear him over the music and the bar's rowdy clientele. "You've heard of the O'Rourkes?"

Everyone had heard of the O'Rourkes. The infamous family ran an import/export business as its legitimate front, which was a cover for a highly successful and illegal drug-smuggling business that seemed to grow bigger every year. The business was based out of Chicago, and even though O'Rourke also had an office in New York, the D.A. had never been able to touch him.

"Of course I've heard of the O'Rourkes," she said, pushing her beer to the side as her head began to pound.

"Well, she's married to one of them. Robert Mercer, Susie's husband, is the guy's son," Sammy said triumphantly. He clinked the neck of his beer bottle with hers.

"Sammy, how did you find that out?" she whispered urgently. Sammy shrugged, unconcerned. Since Susie had come forward, Robert Mercer was under investigation for more than just domestic abuse—the D.A.'s office was trying to keep his connection to the O'Rourkes under wraps until the Grand Jury convened in two weeks. If Sammy confirmed to anyone that Ava now knew the information…

She wanted to shake him by the shoulders until his teeth rattled.

"Now, that's something I can't tell you," he said, before bringing the bottle back to his mouth and draining it.

"You can't tell anybody else about this. Do you understand?"

"Don't worry about me…well, only make sure I get out of trouble. Detective Rumson always says you're the only one in the D.A.'s office who can be trusted."

She stared into the man's eyes and wondered why she

always felt as if there was no one in the world she could trust. "Are you sure there's no word on where Susie is?"

Sammy shook his head. "But if I had to guess, the family got her. There's no way to escape them."

But Susie had escaped. For now she was well hidden, safe and sound. The day after she'd pressed domestic abuse charges against her husband, Ava had helped her get away from her husband, since Susie refused to put her faith in the more conventional witness protection program. Ava had told this to no one, and wouldn't be telling Sammy, either.

It had been reported that Susie's husband, a successful New York entrepreneur, was now the main suspect in her "disappearance." Although Robert Mercer had been under investigation at the D.A.'s office long before Susie had come forward to speak with Ava.

Something bigger was going on here. Robert Mercer's hands were always somehow clean, his business dealings perfect. Still, Ava would make sure Susie's case was solid, one way or the other.

With the help of Callie, she'd also make sure Robert never got anywhere near Susie again.

Callie was a social worker with close ties to the D.A.'s office, especially concerning domestic abuse cases, and an ally who'd helped Ava assist more women in peril than she could ever have imagined.

Callie was part of the backbone of an underground railroad that helped women get away from their abusive mates and into a new life. A program run entirely by volunteers, including some of the most unlikely people Ava would have ever expected. And, as each woman had been helped, she'd become the next important link in the chain.

It was the most important work Ava had ever done.

You'll be straddling the legal line, Callie warned her when she'd first approached Ava about helping those women the system had failed, the ones whose husbands weren't prosecuted. The ones who'd rather escape than face their tormentor in open court.

With this case, Ava had crossed it. There was no turning back now.

FIFTEEN MINUTES FROM Ava's house, Justin pulled his cell phone from his pocket and made the call he'd been dreading.

"Where are you?" Rev, his SEAL teammate, yelled into the phone, over the sounds of loud music. Which meant he was still in the bar, where Justin had left him and the rest of the team, including Cash, earlier in the evening.

"I'm, ah, in a situation," he said.

"Yeah, we saw you leave the bar with that situation well in hand." Rev chuckled at his own wit and Justin thought about hanging up now and saving himself.

"I had to go to New York," he said instead, ignoring his better judgment not to give him details because it was all shot to hell anyway. He'd need his team—no, his friends—to know where he was, just in case. If he couldn't trust them, he had nothing.

"New York? He's in New York!" Rev yelled, and Justin could only pray that he wasn't telling Cash. Anyone but Cash, because if Cash heard New York...

"Is this about Ava?" Cash demanded. Justin heard Rev grumbling in the background, no doubt because Cash mowed him down to get to the phone and dammit, Cash was supposed to be spending time with his girlfriend.

Cash was Justin's best friend on the team—the one Justin confided in the most. The one who Justin had watched fall in love hard last year with a documentary filmmaker named

Rina. And although Hunt and Rev both knew about his past with Ava, Cash was the only one who knew exactly how many regrets Justin still had.

"I thought Rina was in town," he said, mentioning Cash's girl-friend as if this was a normal, everyday conversation and he was not having to admit to being minutes away from facing his past.

"Her flight from Botswana got canceled. Engine trouble. She's coming in tomorrow night. And don't try and change the subject."

"Turk called me. Ava's in trouble. Big trouble," he said finally.

"Yeah. Always is. And now, I'm sure you are, too."

"Just put Rev back on the phone," Justin said, without telling his friend that this particular brand of Ava trouble had the potential to be bigger and badder than ever. Cash did so, but Justin could still hear him cursing a blue streak. In Swahili.

"What's going on?" Rev asked.

"Can you go to my house and make sure it's tight?" he asked, because Rev was the security master of the group.

Rev was silent for a minute. "CG?" he asked, and yes, that was the code—code green—they'd developed for when something really bad was going down and they couldn't say much about it.

"Yeah. I'm not sure when I'll be back. Probably by tomorrow night—late."

"Consider it done," Rev said. "Once I figure out why my car won't start."

Justin groaned and hung up, because, even though he knew Rev would take care of what he needed to, it wouldn't come without a certain amount of high drama and last-minute tension Rev seemed to have a penchant for.

Justin turned the corner slowly, parked a few houses down from Ava's. It was nearly one in the morning. He'd been able to catch a military flight that got him here inside of an hour. But first he'd do a quick sweep to make sure everything was all right before ringing her doorbell and making contact... when Ava, still driving that same Mustang convertible Turk and her father had rebuilt for her ages ago, pulled into the driveway.

Within seconds she was striding toward the front door of her house, dressed in a pair of well-worn but still formfitting jeans, a white, V-neck T-shirt and a pair of high-heeled black boots that were part sex kitten, part Harley mama and every man's fantasy. Including his.

She'd been hot enough at seventeen to make him crazy. Apparently nothing had changed if the way his pulse was racing was any indication.

Spending any decent amount of time with her had always made him feel as if he should be hoisting the white flag of surrender, although he was never quite sure what he was surrendering to.

He could run fifteen miles in one shot without a problem. Uphill, in the rain and carrying a pack that weighed eighty pounds or with one of his teammates slung over his shoulder. Swim in oceans so rough that drowning sometimes seemed the easier option. Been shot at more often than he cared to remember and still, seeing her could take him down at the knees every single time.

He'd spent the better part of his eighteenth year bailing her out of various scrapes—and honky-tonks, telling himself he was doing it for Turk and Ava's father the entire time. Gotten into more than a few old-fashioned, chair-throwing, window-breaking bar fights with guys who'd wanted to take her home. And done more than his share of locking her in her room so she could study and wouldn't fail her classes.

He'd only made the mistake of locking her in and standing outside her door once. He'd been so proud of her two hours of straight study, without complaint, until he'd gotten a call from the police about a woman caught speeding. On his hog.

When he'd gone to collect her from the precinct, she'd been unapologetic. Just smiled and batted those eyelashes and he'd wanted to kill her. And kiss her, too. And she'd known it. Always had.

He was never sure if that made things better or worse.

Ava, with her fierce loyalty and strong sense of justice, even then, she probably could've helped him, but at the time…

At the time, he couldn't face her. He'd called her from a pay phone outside the motel where he was staying and explained why he wasn't at her graduation when, the night before, they'd rolled together on the floor of her room. When he'd nearly taken her for the first time—her first time. A night when he'd had to tell her he was marrying someone else.

He'd told himself that he called because he hadn't wanted her to see the bruises on his face, to ask too many questions.

He called because he couldn't stand seeing the look on her face, the one of disappointment that he'd never wanted to put there. The one he'd seen when she recalled her mother leaving, and then firsthand when her father died and again when Turk announced he was transferring to an out-of-state college on a scholarship.

He'd called because he'd been leaving her, too.

Now, from the safety of the car, he watched the sway of her hips, wondered if her hair still smelled like that flowery shampoo she used to use. Wondered if she still hated him as much as she had that night.

He'd find out soon enough.

AVA WAS DEEP in thought as she approached her front door. It took three tries to get the key into the lock because her mind was racing due to Sammy's news. And, if she was honest with herself, because her hands were shaking slightly. The O'Rourkes were getting too close—to Susie…to everything.

She'd have to let the detectives know about this development, could, in fact, since it wasn't attorney-client privilege. And lie, the way she'd been doing for the past months when women like Susie Mercer disappeared off the face of the earth…

Susie planned to come back into town to give her grand jury statement and what evidence she could against her husband—and now presumably the O'Rourkes, too—in less than two weeks. She had evidence of the domestic abuse she'd suffered as well as the corrupt business dealings of her husband, and she was ready and willing to testify about both matters. She'd told both Ava and Callie not to worry about getting her back into New York, that she just needed their help in getting out. Susie refused to trust the police, the FBI and the federal marshals. She told Ava and Callie that if she was putting her life on the line, she was going to do it her way.

When Ava finally got the door open, she pushed in and noticed something by her feet.

A plain white envelope had been slipped through the mail slot in her door. She stared at it for a moment because there was no name or address on the front. And then she slid a finger under the sealed edge and ripped it open impatiently.

Photographs slid out. Polaroids of her in various places over the course of the last couple of days. Entering her office. Sitting with Susie. Going to dinner.

Meeting with Sammy tonight at the bar.

She fought the revulsion curling in her stomach and stuffed

the pictures back into the envelope. No fear. *Don't let the bastards get to you.*

God, she'd been outside—right in the open…

She moved fully into the foyer and slammed and locked the door behind her. Instinctively, she pulled the .38 special she'd started carrying, at Leo's insistence, from her bag and held it at the ready while she turned on all the lights on the first floor. And then wondered if that was such a good idea.

She forced herself to stand still, to calm down and think. She could handle this.

She'd pack a bag, head straight for the anonymity of the city, hand the pictures over to the police and stay in a hotel. She'd be safe then.

Callie's words of wisdom echoed in her head.

If anything happens, leave your place for a while. Go anywhere. And don't tell anyone where you're going…

Panic washed over her. That didn't happen often, but the feeling in the pit of her stomach grew worse with each passing minute.

She wouldn't worry about packing—she could come back here with the police tomorrow for her things. She shoved the pictures into her bag and opened the front door. And screamed.

"Jesus, Ava—what's with the gun, are you trying to kill me?"

Justin. Justin filled the doorway, his hand poised as if readying to knock. Her breath caught and she was frozen in place at the sight of him.

He didn't appear to be having the same problem. Barging past her, he insisted, "Ava, talk to me. Are you all right?"

Was she all right? No, not by a long shot.

"Justin, I'm in trouble," she sputtered, because she couldn't think of anything else to say, because she was scared and half in shock. The last person in the world she'd expected to find on her doorstep was Justin Brandt, but he might be the only one who could give her what she needed right now.

"I won't let anything happen to you, but you have to put the gun *down*." His drawl was thick and familiar, comforting, even as she realized the gun was still pointed at his chest.

"Sorry."

Justin glanced behind Ava and then gave her a firm but gentle push aside with one hand. The other held her hand with the gun pointed downward. He kept his hand on that arm, even after he closed the door.

He was standing so close, and for a second, just a second, she forgot the danger and everything else but the heat of his body. Justin looked even better with some years on him. Bigger, stronger, faster. Her hero. Big and blond, with dark eyes so intense they could melt her. So handsome, he made her ache, and the nine years they hadn't seen each other disappeared.

"Did your brother call you?" he asked, his eyes lingering on hers for a brief moment before he was scanning the parts of the house that he could see from the foyer.

"No. Not for three months. Have you spoken with Leo? Is he all right?" The words rushed out of her and she didn't bother worrying about putting up a brave front. She never had to do it with Justin. He'd seemed to always understand that she was brave even when she wasn't in control.

"He was breathing," Justin said wryly. It was an old joke the three of them used to share with Ava's father. Obviously it was meant to calm her. "And he's just as worried about you. What's going on here?"

She'd tell him what she could, as little as possible without having his human lie detector Navy SEAL instincts kick into high gear. "I'm trying to figure that out myself."

She shoved the pictures at him and began to pace in the small hallway, which was made much smaller by Justin's presence. He flipped through them quickly, shaking his head and muttering, nothing she could make out, but she knew when Justin muttered they were usually words that could make a sailor blush.

"Who is this guy?" he demanded.

"My informant. He was helping me out on my current case."

"Your informant sold you out."

"No. He wouldn't do that."

"He's not a criminal, then?"

"He gave me crucial information. Why would he do that and then betray me?"

"Where is he now?"

"I left him at the bar a while ago. I told him not to tell anyone. To be careful."

Justin stared at her. "This picture was *just* taken?"

"Yes. That's why I was leaving. To go straight to the police," she lied, but Justin was shaking his head.

"No, not tonight. What happened with your informant tonight sounds like a setup."

Until Justin said it, she hadn't wanted to believe it. Now she was completely unsure whether or not Sammy would have gotten the scoop on the Mercers if there hadn't been a direct purpose. "If that's true, then they've been watching me."

"Any idea why?"

Several. Nothing, however, that she could share freely.

"It's because of my current case. It has to be. Does Leo know about it?"

"I don't know what he knows. He called, said I needed to get you out of town, and he didn't elaborate."

Out of town sounded really good, but Justin would expect her

to put up more of a fight. "I don't know if I can leave like this—
I have a job. Responsibilities. People who are counting on me."

Justin had already opted for the most effective argument.
"Leo wouldn't ask you to do anything if he didn't have
specific reason to. And I know you trust your brother."

"Yes. Of course I trust him."

Justin stared at her with those dark eyes filled with an
emotion she couldn't put her finger on. "More importantly,
right now, you've got to trust me."

"Trust was never *my* issue." She said it before she could
stop herself and he blanched visibly, as though she'd physically struck him.

"I guess you think I deserve that." His voice was tight as
he continued. "Maybe I do, but you shouldn't ever question
my commitment to keeping you safe."

She didn't question that. Justin was the best at what he did,
according to Leo.

Her father had been a dangerous man. Leo was one too,
and even though she'd always known, on some level, that
Justin was an equal to both men in her family, she hadn't had
the opportunity to see it until then. She could sense the
predator in him as he stood before her, fully on her side. But
there was nothing to say her heart was safe.

With Justin, it never had been.

"So, are you with me?" he asked again. "I'm going to need
your full cooperation, Ava. Because Turk didn't give me much
to go on, and I don't really know what we're in for."

"And still, you came all the way here to save me?" she asked
quietly, not sure why it mattered so much. But somehow, it did.

"I came here to honor a request from one of my best
friends," he said, as if it was no big deal, but his jaw tensed,
nearly imperceptibly, letting her know otherwise.

"Leo told me to call you if I got into trouble," she said.

"Then why didn't you?"

"The last time…" She trailed off.

"Yeah, I know." He closed his eyes briefly, as if trying to ward off the pain of the memory of their history. "We can't do this now. Let's do what your brother wants, and then…"

And then…

She couldn't think past the next five minutes, let alone that far ahead. "I can do that," she told him and suddenly she was seventeen and he was eighteen and their future was stretched out in front of them, inextricably linked.

"Come on, we'll figure this out from someplace safer."

"You don't think…I mean, you think I'm really not safe here at all?"

"I think I don't want to wait to find out." He put a hand on the small of her back and guided her to the front door. "Stay behind me, all right? And keep your gun low and not pointed at me."

3

WITH AVA A FEW STEPS behind Justin, hanging on to his belt as he'd told her, they got to his rental car without incident. Still, he did *not* have any good feelings about this one. When a slow-moving car, headlights off, pulled onto the end of the street, he knew he was more than right.

Someone had been waiting for Ava to get home, to make their move on her. Her leaving was not what they had in mind and Justin didn't wait to get the make and model, hear the inevitable, unmistakable sound of gunfire that followed before he peeled away from the curb.

"Stay low, Ava." He automatically pushed her so her body was almost to the floor as one shot then another cracked the back windshield but didn't shatter it. *Shit.*

He careened around the corner, looking to put just enough distance between them to pull into a hiding spot. There wasn't enough traffic this time of night around here to lose the sporty number following them.

Three blocks later, he found what he was looking for, pulled the car between two low sheds and cut the lights and the engine. He prayed, but held his weapon at the ready at the same time because he always found the combination of the two to be the most effective.

Ava, it appeared, was holding her breath. And looking slightly blue. Not really a great color on her.

She was staring at him and he realized that he was motioning for her to breathe in SEALspeak, not Avaspeak. She was looking at him as if he was crazy.

He pulled her close, whispered against her ear, *breathe,* and felt her inhale a huge gulp of air. And then another, in a slightly hitched manner.

She stopped when the sound of another car rounded the corner, headlights momentarily throwing light on their car and hopefully, it was mingling in with the shadows. Ava had moved closer to him unconsciously, and any other time he would've been thrilled with that contact. As it was, she was burrowing against the arm that held the gun, making it impossible to move without flinging her unceremoniously to the floor. Which he'd do if he had to, but she'd definitely be unhappy with him.

She also had a lot more explaining to do than just, *this all has to do with my current case.* But he was skilled enough in interrogation to know that she'd tell him everything he needed to know one way or another. Having a history with her helped in that regard.

Of course, she also knew him well, too.

Slowly, excruciatingly slowly, the car pulled away.

She looked slightly shaken, but she was breathing and there was no blood. And she wasn't staring up at him with that goddamned "you're my hero" look he was pretty familiar with after he rescued someone on the job, which was good. He didn't want hero worship from her.

What do you want from her?

The truth, he told himself firmly. And for a minute, he almost believed it.

AVA CLUTCHED Justin's arm as she strained to listen for any signs of the other car's return.

Her palm ached from where she'd held the gun so tightly,

her heart beat faster as the earlier scene began to replay itself in her head. She couldn't get past the sound of shots being fired, wouldn't make the mistake of staring out the rear window that had been struck by a pair of bullets. It was one thing to practice shooting at a range and entirely another to be in the line of fire.

She much preferred the former and realized that the breathing thing was getting harder.

"Put your head between your legs and try to take deep breaths. In through your nose, out through your mouth," Justin was explaining, but his voice sounded far away, his drawl more pronounced…his large palm against her cheek.

What seemed like seconds later, mainly because that palm was less than gently slapping her cheek, she opened her eyes with a start. Her seat had been pushed all the way back and her gun was gone.

His hand shifted from her cheek to her neck, then reached down for her hand. For a second, she thought he was going to hold it.

"Your pulse is still racing," he said, finger firmly on the point at her wrist. "You should stay down for a while."

And then, for just a second, he did put his hand in hers, giving it a light squeeze. His hand was big, reassuring, and if she pretended hard enough she could actually believe that there was something more in his touch than mere comfort.

When he took his hand away, she shifted to face him. "Did we lose them?" she asked, her voice hoarse as if she'd been screaming out loud for hours. In reality, she hadn't, but inside her head she was still yelling.

"For now." His voice was intense, his drawl nearly nonexistent.

"So why aren't we moving?"

"We'll have to sit for a while. They'll circle around until they're sure we've disappeared." He glanced at the empty neighborhood. "I've also got to lose this car and these plates."

"Around here? You're going to steal a car?"

"I prefer to think of it as borrowing," he said. "And no, not here, we'll have to make do with this one for a while longer. At least until we get out of state."

"Where are we going?"

"I was going to take you down to my place, in Norfolk, but I don't know if that's such a good idea." His hand, which had been playing along the steering wheel gripped it tighter, the muscle in his forearm flexed and she noted again how much bigger he'd gotten. All filled out—no more signs of the young man she'd known in high school. His hair was shorter now, but still as blond and he was still tanned, too.

He took a deep breath, as if he'd made a decision. "We'll drive for a few hours, then stop before dawn. Rest, regroup. Decide what our next move should be. Until we know more about who's threatening you, I don't want you to have any contact with your office."

"No one in the D.A.'s office has anything to do with this," she insisted, but her voice sounded worried, even to her own ears.

"Unless you're one hundred percent sure, I'm not taking any chances. Not when I promised your brother I'd take care of you until he could." He paused. "What's this new case all about?"

"It's a domestic abuse case. I've prosecuted cases like this before and yes, I've been threatened before." She gave him the pat answer, the easy answer.

"Like this?"

She bit her bottom lip and nodded. "Abusive husbands often try to control me the way they control their wives. I can't let them win. I made a commitment to these women, to help them. Do you know how long it's taken some of them to come forward, to finally trust someone?"

"I can only imagine." His voice was tight again, and maybe, just maybe, he'd understand. At least she thought so until he spoke. "But you can't put your life on the line for every case."

"Does your SEAL team have that same motto?" she asked, and his lips pressed together in a grim line. "You don't get to tell me what I can and can't do, Justin."

"In this case, I do. You're going to need to listen to me, Ava." And with that he straightened up and turned the key in the ignition.

She guessed his internal timeframe had told him it was safe to leave. Still, she noted that he didn't switch on the car's headlights until they were on the highway, headed southbound. "I'm doing all this for your own good."

How many times had she heard that in her lifetime, from Justin, Leo, her father…even her mother?

She'd had no idea an hour ago that when she opened her door she'd be opening up the door to her past.

AVA HAD HER CELL PHONE out and she was dialing. And ignoring him and his advice. Just like old times. Which, in a way, was good. It meant she was bucking up under the pressure, that she wouldn't completely fall apart. Yet.

He grabbed the phone from her. "What are you doing? You just agreed we weren't going to tell anyone anything," he said.

"I want to talk to Leo," she said. "I want to talk with someone in the DEA office. If they know anything—anything at all that's related to why my life's at risk—I deserve to know." She kicked the dashboard in frustration. Twice. Which made the front end of the POS rental car rattle.

"I know you do," he said, trying to talk her down from the emotional ledge she'd worked herself onto.

"Maybe in your world having men shoot at you isn't a big deal—"

"It's always a big deal," he said through gritted teeth. He shifted his hands on the steering wheel and then took a breath. She was shaken, badly, and when Ava was thrown off her game she reacted by lashing out at the nearest available person. Which, in high school, always seemed to be him.

But this wasn't high school. They were all grown up and this was all too damn real. "I need you to tell me everything that happened to you today. You can start with the informant, or think back, if there was anything else out of the ordinary that happened. Maybe something you'll only notice in hindsight…did you feel like you were being followed? Have you been seeing the same man for the past few days and thought it was just one of those weird coincidences?"

"No, I hadn't noticed anything out of the ordinary. I've just been working—ninety-hour weeks. I barely have time to lift my head and notice the world around me."

That was Ava. She'd always thrown herself headfirst into whatever her cause or interest had been. Like a whirlwind, she gave all her time, devotion and energy until she'd completed the latest project to her satisfaction.

"You've got to tell me everything you know about this case you're working on," Justin insisted.

"I shouldn't be telling you any of it."

"Under typical circumstances, I'd respect the need for confidentiality. But this has gone way beyond that—I need to know what we're up against."

Ava stared out the windshield as she told him about Susie

and Robert Mercer in halting words, as though she was trying not to give away more than necessary.

"So you met with the informant, he tells you that your newest client, who's disappeared off the face of the earth, is the wife of a man who's the son of one of the biggest drug traffickers—which is information you already knew. And then you come home to find pictures of yourself."

"That about sums it up," she said. "It's not good that Sammy has that information—it's not good that he knows that I know who Robert Mercer really is. Before this, the D.A.'s office was only supposed to know about the domestic abuse charge. My boss didn't want us to give away our hand, not until the police and the federal marshals got involved."

She was looking down at her hands, her nails short, manicured with a light, no-nonsense polish, but he'd bet anything that her toes were painted a fire-engine red, or maybe purple. Something unexpected under all the logic.

He had the nagging sense that she was holding something back, but he let it go for the moment. "Did you tell him that?"

"I did. He refused to tell me where he'd gotten the information." She shook her head. "He's low level…I don't know why someone would just offer up that tidbit to him."

"He could've been in the right place at the right time."

"Or it was a giant setup, like you said before. A way to get me out of the house." She paused. "A way to scare the hell out of me."

Ava might be scared now, but what these men didn't realize was that the fear wouldn't last long, it'd be replaced quickly by her natural fighting instincts.

"We'll stop just before dawn," he said. "I'm going to have to figure out what to do with this car. I can't be sure someone didn't see us leave. I don't know if the guys who came after you were watching your house."

"I'm not sure of anything anymore," Ava whispered before she turned away from him to stare out the window into the darkness.

WHEN LEO HAD FIRST gotten wind that Susie Mercer had gone to the D.A.'s office to file a charge of domestic abuse, then also confessed to knowing her husband's dealings with the O'Rourke family and refused federal protection, he'd wanted to bang his head against the wall.

When he found out Ava was lead counsel for the prosecution for both the domestic abuse charge and the possible indictment of Robert Mercer for being involved with the O'Rourkes, he did just that. Twice. And the headache that followed was nothing compared to the way his head pounded now.

The D.A.'s office didn't realize that their secret information regarding Mercer's hidden criminal connection wasn't nearly as secret as they thought.

As he slid his leather jacket on, he wondered if he'd ever be able to recognize himself in the mirror again. Too much scruff on his face, hair too long, a far cry from his usual suit and tie, official DEA office wear.

You wanted undercover. Be careful what you wish for.

He'd gotten bored with the usual action, the paperwork. The bullshit bureaucracy that seemed to haunt every one of his work assignments while he slammed through the ranks.

Hearing about Justin's travels all over God's green earth hadn't quelled his instincts to play hard and work even harder. Turk had known military life wasn't for him, but he'd been surprised at just how badly he'd wanted to take a walk on the darker side of life.

He hadn't wanted to take his sister down that path with him, had been glad when she'd refused to work for the DEA as one of their team of lawyers, no matter how hard they'd tried to recruit her.

When he made contact with his office yesterday he'd received the news that Ava was on the Mercer case, looking to put the people he'd been investigating for months behind bars, but on charges that wouldn't stick without the information the DEA had been carefully gathering.

The link between Robert Mercer and the O'Rourke clan was little known outside the tight-knit world Leo had infiltrated. Until Susie had come forward with a domestic abuse claim—and Robert Mercer had panicked.

The O'Rourkes hadn't panicked. They planned on doing what they did best—protecting their own interests by trying to grab Susie first.

Except that Susie Mercer suddenly went missing and couldn't be located through FBI, or any of the other law enforcement agency channels.

On the O'Rourke estate, Leo heard rumors that O'Rourke's men had orders to kill whoever was assisting Susie or would be closely involved with a possible trial.

He wasn't sure what else to do but call in Justin.

He trusted Justin with his life, with Ava's, but this was bigger than all of them and more dangerous than the DEA had originally conceived.

Anyone going after Ava would have had to have researched her family. Leo'd taken precautions but hadn't exactly erased himself…if they'd gone through Ava's house, seen pictures…

It was a leap, but not a huge one. Once he knew Ava was in his buddy's care, he could relax momentarily, move to the next phase of his job and figure out the rest later.

4

JUST BEFORE THREE in the morning, they crossed the border from Pennsylvania into Maryland. Justin steered the car onto an exit ramp. Nearby a sign boasted lodging.

Ava had waited in the car while he went into the front office and got them a room, and then he'd driven them around the back of the motel, to a room on the first floor.

The room, the entire motel, left a lot to be desired, but they were in no position to be picky. At least it was clean, tacky orange and brown furnishings aside.

Justin was doing something to the front door of the room with wires, and she didn't bother to ask what.

"You'll probably want something more comfortable to sleep in. You can grab a shirt and shorts from my bag," he told her without turning around from what he was doing.

They hadn't spoken much during the past hour of their trip. She'd been so wrapped up in the mounting enormity of her situation and he was, no doubt, angry with her. Now, as she rifled through his bag and pulled out some clothes, the reality of what had happened began to hit home.

In the privacy of the bathroom she contemplated the sudden and complete train wreck her life had become in less than four hours, thought about the work she'd left behind—all her cases, all her clients…Callie…

It had been a long time since Ava had had any close female friends, if she ever really had them at all. In high school, the girls all wanted to be friends with her because of Leo and Justin, so she hadn't trusted them. During college, she'd put her nose to the grindstone so she could graduate a year early, and although she'd had her share of dates, getting close to anyone hadn't been her priority.

But when she'd met Callie last year, the women had clicked immediately. Callie loved her job and had, in a roundabout way, begun to help Ava love what she was doing again as well.

She'd confided in Callie about her love life. About Justin and a fiancé who'd given her an ultimatum. And so, for the first time in forever when she actually had a girlfriend she could confide in, Ava wasn't even able to reach out to her for help.

She could only reach out to Justin.

As she'd stripped off her T-shirt and jeans, she realized she was shivering again.

She wasn't going to fall apart, not when there was so much on the line.

She put the shorts on first, then pulled Justin's T-shirt over her head, pausing for a minute to smell the combination of freshly laundered shirt that still contained a hint of the Justin she remembered, like fresh air and raw, uninhibited energy.

Justin was sitting in the chair across from the bed, waiting for her. "Don't touch the windows or the door," he warned. "They're alarmed."

"Okay," she said, grateful at the moment that Justin was some kind of one-man army. Navy. Whatever.

"Are you hungry? Thirsty? I could run out and get you something…"

"No." She shook her head, almost wishing Justin wasn't treating her with such kid gloves.

"You should get some sleep, then." He'd drawn the curtains tightly. She'd never have known the sun was just dawning.

"I'm a little too keyed up to sleep," she admitted. "There's so much I left behind, so much unfinished."

"I heard you were engaged," he said suddenly. "Will your fiancé be worried about you? Will he alert the police?"

"We're taking a break," she said, and Justin was silent for a second. "He's not even in the country," she added, because Justin still wasn't saying anything.

"Oh. Okay." He paused, then asked, "He's a desk jockey, isn't he?"

"Not everyone has the desire to be a big, bad Navy SEAL. But if you must know, he's a commodities trader. He moved to Japan for a year and he wanted me to go with him." He'd given her a ring after two months of dating, even though she'd protested. After five months of her duck-and-run routine, he'd gotten tired and taken the job. And she'd returned the ring.

"Okay."

"Could you stop saying okay?"

"Why didn't you go with him?" he asked instead, and suddenly she realized that okay was much, much better.

"Because I'm not following someone around the globe. I have my own life. Subject closed."

"Fine."

"Fine?"

"I'd go back to okay, but that seems to annoy you," he said. And he was smiling a bit, with that still-familiar look he always gave her—the look she hadn't been able to forget, a cross between amusement and indulgence. It was the indulgence part she'd always counted on. The part he probably didn't even know he was giving away.

It was nice to have at least something on him because

truthfully he drove her crazy. This was treacherous territory. Heartbreaking.

Nine years should be long enough for anything to fade, but it had never been easy between them. And with both she and her brother in trouble, difficult was par for the course.

JUSTIN SWORE he could hear the wheels in Ava's head spinning at full speed. She nibbled her bottom lip, and suddenly there it was—the serious look on her face tempered by the freckles on her nose and cheeks, and a gleam in her eye that meant she could never, ever be tamed.

He knew people would spend a lifetime trying anyway.

He never got why someone would want to restrain something so free and wild. Run it a bit, harness it, yes, he got that. He'd tried to help where Ava was concerned, do his part, until she'd started to resent him and he got tired of being the daddy and everything blew up in their teenage faces.

That would happen again if he didn't start pulling it together and figuring out what to do next.

He refused to let it happen. Not this time. He didn't want to head back to base with his tail between his legs and admit to his friends and SEAL teammates, like Hunt and Rev, the extent of his longing. Well, Cash knew already.

"How do you do this?" She'd begun to pace like a caged animal. "How do you just sit around and wait?"

"Normally, I'm on the offensive. In the field. I don't babysit for a living," he said quietly. "I know it's frustrating. But right now, the best thing we can do is get you out of harm's way and let Turk do his job." He saw her eyes soften a bit at the mention of her brother.

"Do you think we'll hear from Leo?" she asked.

"Probably not. It's better that way."

"But he's got the DEA backing him, right?"

"Yes," Justin said patiently, but he knew she wouldn't trust what he said fully. She knew better. The world of undercover operations wasn't always a play-by-the-rules type of situation, and the very fact that Turk had sent Justin in meant her brother could possibly be in way over his head.

She stared him down hard. "Do you ever go on missions where no one's backing you? No ID, nothing?"

"You know I can't answer that."

"Yes, I know. Classified. You and Leo are all sorts of classified," she muttered.

"Just like you and your current case," he tried to refute, tried to bring it around to something she could understand.

"That's different, and you know it," she countered. "You can't protect me forever."

"Do you think I want to do this? Do you think I want to spend the rest of my life cleaning up after you?" He struggled to keep his voice tight, controlled. Stay rational.

"I stopped knowing what you wanted years ago. And I never asked you to clean up after me. That was always my father and Leo's doing."

"*I* never knew what you wanted," he said, aware that he couldn't hide the anger. "You never did either—that was a big part of the problem between us."

"Us?" She laughed, a slightly hysterical sound. "There was never any us, Justin. That was the real problem."

Her words hit him harder than he thought they would, harder than they should have. Maybe they'd never gotten together, but that hadn't been from lack of want on his part. No, he'd had to tread lightly around Ava for many reasons— she was the sister of his best friend, she'd become one of his best friends…she hadn't wanted to get serious with anyone who was considering a career more dangerous than sitting at a desk. She'd told him that, time and time again.

There was never any us, Justin.

No, there was no way he'd ever believe that. He might never have done anything about it, but that had been for her benefit, not his. He'd promised himself he'd never come back into her life when he couldn't give her what she wanted—someone safe.

"I know you're hurt—upset. Scared, even. But don't you dare sit there and try and tell me there was never anything between us, Ava." His words came out fierce, without reservation. Her green eyes were wide as she watched him. But he strode over and turned the light out because he couldn't look at her anymore, couldn't stand to see the pain there. "Get some sleep. We've got a long stretch ahead of us."

For once, she didn't argue with him. He heard the shift of the blankets as she lay down, but he knew sleep wouldn't come easily for either of them anytime soon.

CALLIE STANTON unconsciously twirled a strand of long, dark hair around her finger while she pored over the case files she'd brought home with her. Great companionship on a Friday night.

Not that she had many other choices.

Another long night faced her, and she'd already gone through her share of Diet Coke in an attempt to keep her eyes from drifting shut again. Sighing, she repositioned herself on the couch since her feet were starting to fall asleep.

She should be happy for the downtime, when she wasn't racing to help anyone, when she wasn't headed to the hospital to counsel a victim. Or worse. But she knew exactly why she wasn't content.

This was the time the loneliness hit her the hardest, like a sudden, sharp ache, so fierce she actually had to force a breath in and out.

One day, my prince will come...

Her mom used to sing that song as she would twirl around the small kitchen of the brand-new apartment, the one she'd rented for them after they'd left Callie's abusive father. At the time, it had been forever since she'd heard her mother sing, let alone smile. In that tiny room, it was as if she'd been reborn.

Callie's mom never remarried, but she did date and finally ended up with a man who loved her to pieces.

Callie never allowed herself to open up as easily. Between her past and the jobs she held, the day job and the secret one, she probably never would.

The sudden, loud knocking at the door did what the caffeine was supposed to as the thumping in her chest could attest to. Hesitantly, she went and looked out the peephole.

Men in suits.

"What do you want?" she called through the heavy apartment door.

"FBI, ma'am. You're going to need to come with us."

Her skin chilled and she prayed this had nothing to do with Susie's case. "For what reason?"

"Ava Turkowski," was all they said, all they needed to say, before she unlocked the door and swung it wide open.

"Is she all right?"

"She's missing. You need to come with us, ma'am," one of the men repeated.

Ava. Missing. *Not good.*

She grabbed her keys, shoved her feet into her old sneakers, glad she was still dressed in the jeans and button-down shirt she'd worn that day.

"I'm ready," she said. And really, she thought she was always ready for anything.

The night air was humid for this time of year, and she wished she'd brought something to tie her hair up.

From her youngest days, the middle of the night had always been her favorite time. The insanity of the day dissipated, but the new day had not yet formed and there were endless possibilities. Things that could go right.

Yeah, and one day, your prince will come.

After she was roughly pushed inside the town car, she realized that it was most definitely not her horse-drawn carriage.

5

AVA HAD FINALLY fallen asleep, although she stirred frequently. Justin had no doubt that, even in her slumber, her mind worked overtime.

He ran his hands through his hair, left them there to press against his scalp to see if that would help alleviate some of the pounding. His life flashing before his eyes, pressure that was accumulating in his skull, began the moment he'd taken Ava from her house.

"Justin," Ava whispered. He hadn't realized she'd been awake, sitting up in bed, watching him in the dim light that flickered out from the bathroom.

"Are you okay?"

"No. Neither are you."

He laughed, but there was absolutely no humor behind it. It was one of those times where her knowing him so well was both a detriment and a relief. "We'll get through this—figure it all out," he said. Every part of him wanted to stretch out on the bed next to her, hold her. Make love to her until the pain went away. Show her that, *dammit,* there was something between them. There always would be.

Except that would be the worst thing he could possibly do now. Talk about complicating things even more, because where would that leave them? It wasn't as if he was leaving the SEALs, at least not willingly. His career would always be too big a barrier between them for anything to work.

He walked over to the closet, took the extra blanket and pillow and spread out on the floor next to the bed, between Ava and the door.

But she protested. "You need sleep just as much as I do, and the floor's not going to be comfortable."

"I'll be fine down here." He'd slept on worse. Much worse. Gone without much sleep for longer than a human being should. Pushed his limits to the max.

Sleeping on the floor next to Ava's bed—talk about a trip down memory lane. Even though he had more than one place he could sleep in Turk and Ava's house, like the living-room couch or Turk's floor, he always found himself in Ava's room on her yellow carpet.

Somehow, in the dark of night, when they were alone and weren't sparring over silly things, he could almost imagine that they could make a go of it. And then he'd remember, like he did now, that Ava didn't want to be with anyone who was planning on going into the military. By that point, he'd already made his decision to enlist.

"Justin?"

"Yes?"

"Why wouldn't the O'Rourkes just kill me?" Her voice held equal parts fear and anger. "How would Leo know any of this?"

Justin had already considered the hows and whys, sitting here in the semidarkness, watching Ava toss and turn a few feet away from him.

She was in danger, and so was his oldest and best friend in the entire world.

Especially now. Getting Ava out of town might have made things even worse for Turk at this point.

Justin took a deep breath and told her something he'd been avoiding. "Your brother mentioned something about his cover."

He heard her suck in a quick breath. "Leo's involved with the O'Rourkes?"

"He didn't say that."

"He didn't have to."

"This isn't your fault," he said. "You were doing your job. You had no idea what you were getting into."

"You still haven't answered my first question."

"I know," he said. He had no doubt that O'Rourke had given the order to kill Ava, and that all of it was a giant warning. A setup for something else much bigger coming down the pike. "You're with me now, nothing's going to happen to you on my watch."

She didn't push again for an answer to her question. More likely than not, she'd come to the same conclusion he had, anyway. "I've caused you so much trouble."

"I can take care of myself." He shifted to try to find a comfortable position, even though he knew there wasn't one. He was too aware of every sound, every change, every nuance.

If anyone tried to get in here, he'd know well in advance. Still, his gun remained at his side. Ava's was on the bedside table, although she hadn't touched it since he'd put it there.

"I guess, out of all those times you'd bailed me out, this has got to be the most complicated," she said.

"The time you went into that biker bar and started asking questions about some guy's alibi and almost got into a fist-fight with the girlfriend was a pretty bad one. Good thing the police came in time."

"Wait a minute. How do you know about that?"

Shit. "Turk told me."

"Leo didn't know that last part. He didn't know about the

police coming. I never told him that. I never told him that I went to the bar. I just told him about the case, since he'd worked undercover with the Hells Angels for a while and I wanted some inside information."

"Oh," was all Justin said, because yes, she'd asked Turk about the motorcycle club and Turk knew his sister well enough to know that she'd march herself into one of the most dangerous bars in upstate New York and nose around. Justin had pulled detail on that one, calling the cops at the last minute rather than trying to take on the entire bar himself.

Actually, he wouldn't have had any problem facing the bar, but yeah, then he would've had to face Ava. Who was staring at him now over the side of the bed the way she used to when they were kids.

"You're the reason all those threats against me mysteriously disappeared. You've been…around all these years."

There was no reason to lie anymore. "I guess I have."

"Why didn't you ever say anything? Stop in and see me?"

"I didn't think you wanted to see me. The fact that you left town the day I got married kind of clued me in."

"Right. The day *after* you kissed me."

No, he wasn't going back there. Already, just the mention of the marriage had made his chest tighten. "I can't do this, Ava. Not now. Not yet." He was still bruised from her earlier words. Plus, he knew she'd find a way to talk about it with him without actually talking about it.

He'd learned a long time ago that talking too much, about any subject, was the fastest way to get into trouble. He'd had a hell of a lot of training in the art of not talking, had been interrogated by some of the best the navy had to offer and beyond, but he still didn't think he could put anything past Ava.

He never was able to hide anything from her, at least not

face-to-face, and the cover of darkness wasn't heavy enough to cloak the damage they'd have to discuss.

AVA SHIFTED in the bed and wished Justin was next to her, wished she'd been able to control her mouth earlier—not one of her finest traits. Justin was right. She was hurt and scared, but she wasn't going to take that out on the man risking everything to help her.

If she still wanted Justin, pushing him away wouldn't accomplish anything. But it had never been easy between them, and with both she and her brother in trouble, it was par for the course.

They'd met on Justin's first day at their high school, a day in mid-September. She'd been a sophomore, her brother a senior and Justin a junior who'd been kicked out of a fancy prep school up north somewhere and returned to Norfolk's public-school system. Leo and Justin had gotten into a knock-down, drag-out fight during gym class that resulted in both of them going first to the E.R., then the principal's office and finally home. They'd each earned a week of suspension.

Justin had been sent over by his father to apologize. Leo was already at the front door, having been coerced by their father to do the same. But before Justin made it to the door, or Leo down the stairs, Ava intercepted. And nothing was ever the same....

She'd been expecting a big ugly bully, or a guy who was so sure of himself that he just oozed creepiness. With the way the girls at school talked about Justin, with a stupid, pathetic look in their eyes as if they'd seen a god or something, she'd been sure she was going to hate him on sight. She always went for brains above beauty.

She had not been expecting a tall blond guy who was more

*handsome than any picture she'd ever seen in any magazine.
Striding up her front walk, he had a determined set to his jaw
and a large, purple bruise, courtesy of her brother, on his left
cheek that did nothing to detract from his rugged good looks.
If anything, that hint of roughness made him look even better.*

*The heat of the Indian summer did not help matters. But
good-looking or not, he'd still hurt her brother. Who, of
course, could more than defend himself, but that still didn't
stop her from marching out the door before Leo could and
down the walk to meet him.*

*"Don't you ever, ever lay a hand on my brother. Do you
understand?" she asked.*

He eyed her calmly. "Are you his bodyguard?"

"I'm his sister."

*"Jesus, Ava, leave it alone." Leo's voice came from over
her shoulder. Her brother put a hand on her arm and pushed
past her. "Hey."*

*"Hey," Justin said, and both boys stuck out their hands at the
same time. She crossed her arms and waited for the I'm sorry
to come out of Justin's mouth, but instead, her brother spoke first.*

*"You want to come in and watch the game?" he asked. Justin
shrugged and soon the two of them were walking up the path
and into the house together, her presence quickly forgotten.*

*That was it? The two of them had nearly killed each other,
over what she couldn't get out of Leo, and certainly Justin
wasn't going to tell her. Or the principal or even her father. And
now, after they'd beaten the crap out of each other, a handshake
was all it took to make them friends? Where was the discussion? The apologies? The promises to never fight again?*

She'd wondered then if she'd ever understand men. Now
she realized that she just wished she understood Justin.
"You're still awake, aren't you?" she asked into the darkness.

"Yes."

"I'm sorry…about before. What I said. I had no right—"

"Forget it."

"I can't forget it, Justin. All these years and I still can't forget it. Can't get it out of my mind that we were supposed to be together."

"How, Ava?" he asked, his drawl thick with emotion. "I don't lead the kind of life you wanted. Even if things hadn't gotten so far off track with my marriage and the baby, I don't know if we would've worked out."

"Please, can you just get into this bed?" She hated the pleading tone in her voice, but Justin got it. She felt the mattress shift under his weight, and within seconds he was pressing into her, his strong arms around her. She could deal with anything as long as he stayed by her side.

Ava nuzzled her face against his shirt, felt his jeans rub against her nearly bare legs. Felt his arousal at her belly and despite everything else, a shiver of desire ran through her.

"Sorry," he whispered, and she wasn't sure if he was apologizing for his arousal or what she'd been through that night— or their past.

Right now, lying next to him, none of it mattered. Tentatively, she brushed her lips on the bare skin above the collar of his T-shirt. He started against her touch. Hadn't expected the intimacy. But he didn't pull back.

She did it again, heard a low rumble rise from his throat and felt his arousal press—impossibly hard—at her belly.

He was watching, waiting for her next move.

"Do you think this is just unfinished business between us?" she asked. "I mean, we came so close…"

So close that she could still feel his weight on her, the nap of her bedroom rug scratching her bare back. She'd thought, before that night, that being naked with Justin might be weird, but there had been nothing strange about it. It had been so good…so right.

So close…

"We've got a lot unfinished between us, but I don't think this is the time to finish it."

"Maybe it's the best time."

"And maybe it's not meant to be at all." He spoke quietly, firmly, but he didn't move away from her.

"Will you tell me what happened, one day?"

"One day," he said. "I'll take care of everything. Your brother will finish his job and all of this mess will be sorted out. In the meantime…"

"In the meantime, will you just hold me?"

There was a pause, and then the bed shifted slightly, so he was on his back and she could rest her head against his chest.

"Don't worry. Your virtue's safe," he joked softly.

"*My* virtue isn't the one you should be worried about."

"You're killing me, Ava."

"If you tell me that you haven't thought about me being in your bed once over the last nine years, then you're an even bigger liar than I am."

"And what have you been lying about?"

Everything. About being over you. "Nothing," she whispered.

"Yeah, me too," he whispered back.

6

LEO TURNED on the cold stone floor and groaned softly. His mouth held the metallic taste of blood and his body ached. And it had just been a teaser of what was to come.

If he didn't make contact with the DEA office every forty-eight hours, someone would come extract him. He'd made the call twenty minutes before he'd been grabbed by men who worked for O'Rourke—men Leo had worked side by side with over the past few months during this undercover mission.

Under and alone.

Except he wasn't alone.

"Are you...oh my God, you're really hurt." A woman's voice. Deep and smoky, like a fine whiskey that would burn in a hurts-so-good way going down.

He groaned and tried to pull himself up to lean against the wall, despite the pain, so he could look the woman in the eye. "Did you think I was just taking a nap?"

The woman had long, dark hair. She was probably in her mid-thirties even though she looked much younger. "I don't know anything. These men brought me in and you were already here. I didn't know who you were."

He wasn't sure himself. Was he Leo, the DEA agent, or Leo, part of O'Rourke's merry band of men?

"Who are you?" he asked instead. He wondered if she

walked in here without a struggle because surely he would've awakened to sounds of her screaming.

"My name's Callie. Those men kidnapped me. They said they were with the FBI."

"They're not."

"I figured that out for myself when they forced me into their car," she said with a hint of sarcasm. She didn't seem surprised that she'd been taken. Did she even know exactly who, and what, she was up against?

His gaze strayed to her beautiful, full lips and he paused to consider what they would feel like on his and— Whoa, yeah, he'd definitely hit his head way too hard. Mission, Leo. Remember the mission.

"What else did they say to you?" he asked.

She pressed her lips together and turned toward the door. "I'm a social worker. They think I know where a woman I helped is hiding."

Not good, *not* good, especially if the woman in question was Susie Mercer. He couldn't ask that now and blow anything. "Is there any water?"

"There's nothing in here but us."

His head ached—possible concussion. He hadn't been aware that he'd been sliding back down the wall until Callie was cradling his head in her lap.

"Don't you dare leave me again. I'm scared enough, I don't want to be alone," she told him indignantly. He looked up into those sky-blue eyes and couldn't think how to break this to her.

He chose the easy way. "How do you know that being alone isn't preferable to being alone with me? How do you know I'm not one of the men who locked you in here?"

"I don't," she said. "But I'm guessing you're not in here because they like you a lot."

He snorted. "How long ago did you get here?"

"It's been a couple of hours at least. They took my watch."

O'Rourke's men were going to kill them both. Why they hadn't yet was anyone's guess.

AVA WAS ALONE in the bed when she woke up. It looked like night inside the room, but she knew it was still daytime beyond the pulled curtains. The pillow she held smelled like Justin.

Justin.

The shower was running and she thought about joining him under the hot spray. She hadn't thought about Justin in the shower in a long time.

Liar, she chided herself. She hadn't thought about it, but that hadn't stopped one of her most frustrating, recurring dreams, thanks to the memory of the night she'd spotted him showering at her family's house.

Her seventeen-year-old self had dreamed about that scene from then on. She imagined him sneaking into her room when the house was quiet, still wet, with him knowing she'd watched him.

He'd climb over her body, his mouth devouring hers as his hands began a steady slide down her bare shoulders, along her upper back and finally, stopping at her hips. He'd squeeze gently, then pull her toward him…closer.

She'd imagined his mouth on her everywhere—her breasts, her stomach, between her legs as she'd let the strong orgasm pull her into the dreamlike state, where Justin held her close and they both slept.

When she woke from those dreams she could still feel Justin on her. His weight. His warmth. His strength as he'd pulsed inside of her.

The whole thing was made more intense because of the

time she'd been half-naked beneath him. His kisses, his touch were better than anything she could ever have expected. On the evening of her graduation, the dream had nearly become a reality and for a few hot minutes, Justin had been all hers.

She threw back the covers. As if guided by that same invisible force that always brought her closer to Justin, she found herself at the bathroom door.

The door was ajar and Justin was in the shower, the only thing between them a sheet of frosted glass. Which was nothing. Nothing at all.

"You can come in," he called, and turning away wasn't an option now. She wouldn't be a coward a second time, even if it was only to call his bluff.

"I just needed to brush my teeth…or something," she mumbled. She caught sight of mouthwash and gulped some gratefully. After she did a not-so-graceful spit and rinse, she glanced at her reflection in the mirror. That's when she realized that there wasn't any steam in the bathroom.

The water stopped, the shower door opened and yes, he'd been taking a cold shower. From the looks of things, it hadn't helped at all. And, oh my God, she was staring.

"Sorry."

"Nothing you haven't seen before," he said.

She was about to protest, when he smiled that slow, lazy smile. The one that made him look so devastatingly handsome and was completely deceptive, since there was nothing slow nor lazy about him and she knew exactly what he was talking about.

He knew she'd seen him in the shower at her family's house. It was after Leo's Senior Prom. Justin was only a junior, but he'd been asked to the prom by a senior—a cheerleader. After the dance they'd all ended up back at the Turkowskis'. And with their dates, they'd planned to drive to ιe beach at dawn. Everyone else was downstairs, still ιartying. Except for Justin.

Now, here, present-day Justin was stepping out of the old ιb, even as her memories of the Justin of her past were ιvving up.

"What did you see that night?" he asked, not bothering with ι towel. She thought about handing him one. They were right ιext to her, stacked on a shelf.

Her nipples tightened and then her belly fluttered and she'd ιever been so aware of her body. "You…stroking yourself," ιhe managed to say. "I heard you, over the sound of the ιater…groaning."

"Oh yeah. I remember that." Why was he moving closer? ιVater droplets spilled off his body, ran in rivulets across the tight ιuscles on his chest and this was ridiculous. This was Justin.

Yes, this was Justin and she'd been a fool to think that the ιhemistry that had always burned between them would dis-ιipate if they ignored it.

"You knew I was there?" she asked, although she knew the ιnswer. This situation was impossible to ignore.

"I knew."

At the time, just as she was now, she'd been unable to tear ιerself away. She'd stared at the shower door as if her life ιepended on it. Although she hadn't been able to see anything ιlearly, she had no doubt as to what he was doing while the ιvater rushed over him. She'd seen the slow, steady motion of ιis arm as his hand worked between his legs, and she'd been ιo close to opening the shower door. Too close, with a ιouseful of Turk's friends just downstairs, waiting for Justin ιo they could drive to the shore. Justin's date among them.

That was the only thing that had stopped her. Now there ιvas nothing like that between them.

"Is it warm in here?" she asked him, but again, he only gave her that smile and continued crowding her until the cool water from his body touched her bare arms, soaked through the T-shirt.

Yeah, this part was definitely different than before.

"Did you see me come?"

"You threw your head back and you…howled," she murmured. It had been a magnificent sight and she asked the question she'd wanted to for years. "Who were you thinking about when you came?"

He leaned toward her, more droplets falling on her face, her chest. "You," he breathed. "Was thinking about you, Ava. But you've always known that, too."

HE'D BEEN EIGHTEEN and he'd wanted that night, any night, with Ava, who was bold, smart, funny and beautiful. Ava, who he'd wanted to join him in the shower. That way, Justin could tell his best friend that his sister had made the first move because somehow, that would make everything all right.

She hadn't—not that night. And right now there was nothing more between them but thin cotton that he'd skim off her body in seconds.

His hands were already tugging at the T-shirt's hem. "Why didn't you come into the shower with me back then?"

"I don't know…all those people were downstairs…your girlfriend."

"She wasn't my girlfriend."

"Then you should've been honest with me," she challenged, and he couldn't argue with her.

"There are a lot of things I should've done. And I'm tired of living with the regrets." With that, he brought his mouth down on hers. She didn't resist in the slightest, seemed to be ready for his touch, even grabbed him by the hair to ensure that he didn't think about pulling back from the inevitable.

Like last night, like nine years before, her mouth was sweet, welcoming…hot as hell as her arms wrapped around his shoulders, her fingers digging in as if she wasn't ever letting him go.

He knew this wasn't the time or the place, but none of that mattered, not the way it had last night when he and Ava and the word *naked* seemed like a really bad idea.

What a difference a few hours made.

His body responded instantly with a powerful, primal urge to take her, claim her and protect her all at once.

That all-consuming need burnt through him like fire.

She tasted sweet, *so sweet,* just as he remembered, and he kept his mouth against hers until he could barely breathe. His body screamed for more contact than just kissing. Until he rushed back to his senses.

He broke away abruptly and she took a few quick breaths, then put her hands to her lips. Seeing her staring up at him in complete confusion reminded him of exactly what his job was. The fact that her cell phone had begun to beep in the background like an early-warning signal hadn't hurt either.

AVA'S PHONE signaled that there was a message and that's all it took to put her firmly back into the present situation. She was in hiding. Leo was MIA. And she and Justin were acting without thinking of the consequences.

Dammit.

Before Justin could stop her, she'd pulled away and run to rifle through his bag, where he'd put her phone last night when they were still in the car. The battery was low and she didn't have her charger, so this might be her last chance to check it, and God, it could be Leo.

"Ava, let me listen first," Justin was pleading, but it was too late. The tone of the caller—and his message—was echoing in her ear. It was menacing enough to make her drop the phone, but not until she'd heard the last words: *If you don't produce Susie Mercer in the next forty-eight hours, your brother, Leo, dies. And so does Callie Stanton.*

The phone fell to the carpet with a soft thud and Justin was retrieving it, putting it to his ear to replay the message. His face tightened.

He clicked the phone shut. He'd pulled on clothes hastily. Even his hair was wet but the look on his face made her feel even worse.

"Are you going to tell me who Callie Stanton is?" he asked. "And don't say that you don't know. The caller knew you would."

"She's a social worker. The one who brought Susie to me."

"And that's all."

"Yes, that's all."

"Ava, don't fuck with me now."

"Do you think I'd do that with Leo's life on the line? With Callie's life…" She drew in a breath and asked herself if this feeling of being shattered would ever go away. "I'm going to be sick," she mumbled, and pushed past him into the bathroom.

He was behind her, rubbing her back, telling her it was going to be all right. He wiped her forehead, then the nape of her neck with a cool washcloth, and implored her to just, *breathe,* which she did until the nausea passed.

"Do you think Leo and Callie are together?" she asked finally, her hands still gripping the sides of the sink for support.

"I don't know. Does Callie know where Susie is?"

She turned to stare into his deep brown eyes and told him the absolute truth. "No. And neither do I."

He nodded. "Even if you did, I would never expect you to give her up. Your brother would never want you to do that."

She was glad she didn't have to make that choice for herself. "You need to go help him. You need to go find Leo."

"I can't, Ava. That's not my jurisdiction."

"And I am?"

"This is what he wanted. I can't run off and leave you alone, and I'm not taking you with me. For all we know, that phone call could be a fake."

"And if it's not?" she asked, and saw the pain pass across his face. "We have to do something."

"We will—we are…we're doing what Leo asked. You're going to get dressed and we're going to get the hell out of here."

"What about the car?"

"I took care of that."

"How…?"

He gave her a quick hug. "Better you don't know. Get dressed."

She paused and drew a deep breath. "I'm scared. And I hate being scared."

"There's nothing wrong with being scared. Fear can keep you alive."

"You're scared before your missions?"

He gave her a lopsided smile. "Yes. Every single one," he said, and it was then that she knew for certain her feelings for Justin Brandt went far beyond lust.

EARLIER THAT MORNING, Rev had gotten into Justin's house easily enough without keys. He'd forgotten to ask Cash for them and had been halfway to Justin's before he'd remembered.

You'd think a SEAL would have better security.

There was nothing Rev had come across in his twenty-four

years that he couldn't break into, be it car or house or even a vault. Locks and alarms seemed to melt away under his touch, which had made it very easy for him to get into trouble when he was younger.

Now, two hours later, he was mission accomplished and he and Cash were out on the water, readying for some midmorning fishing so Cash's girlfriend could finish her work.

"I'm not enjoying this." Cash was busy cursing as he tried unsuccessfully to get their CO's boat running.

Hollywood's boat was a beauty—an old AFT Cabin powerboat he'd restored by hand, but she was temperamental as anything and seemed to only want to behave for Hollywood himself. But that didn't mean Rev wouldn't try to tame her every chance he got.

"Can you please let me at the engine now?" Rev asked his friend, knew Cash's temper tantrum had everything to do with Justin.

Cash stepped aside, still swearing. "I hate it when he does this."

"Sees the woman he loves?"

"You know what I mean, Rev. This isn't good for Justin."

"It's the first time he's actually talked with her in a while. Only good can come out of that."

"You sound like a goddamned greeting card."

"And you sound cynical as hell for someone who's in love."

Cash frowned. "I don't want to see him hurt."

"Now who sounds like a greeting card? He's been through much worse. He'll survive this, no matter what the outcome." Rev threaded the band around the motor for the third time, held it so it wouldn't slip off and had it purring in seconds.

The boat cut through the water effortlessly as Rev gunned the engine to get them to the center of the lake.

"That's an awfully long time to hold on to a torch and not do a thing about it," Cash said.

"He had his reasons," Rev replied.

"Do you think feelings can really survive for that long?"

"I think they already have."

"He's not thinking straight, Rev."

"Yeah, well, my papa says that no man who's with the right woman ever does."

7

CALLIE WAS AMAZINGLY resilient. She didn't seem freaked out over his injuries at all. Worried, yes, but Leo knew he looked like hell warmed over. One eye was swollen shut, he wheezed with every breath and his lip was split, yet she just kept talking to him in a low, soothing voice to keep him awake.

She was just easygoing enough for him to know how guarded she really was. Reading people was a big part of his job, but it had always been something that came naturally to him.

And with respect to Callie, there was a story there, and he'd get it soon enough.

"Is anything broken?" she asked as she checked him over with a light touch.

"You're a nurse?"

"No."

"I don't think anything's broken beyond a rib or two. And a cheekbone." They could've hurt him a lot worse, would probably do so when O'Rourke himself got back into Chicago tomorrow night. Unlike most men of his rank in an organization like this, O'Rourke always liked to do the dirty work himself.

Leo really, really hoped Justin had Ava, because this was going to get bad.

"Look, I get that you're in a lot of pain, but we've got to

get out of this place," she told him, her expression so serious
he almost laughed.

"When was the last time anyone came in here?"

"Not since I was brought in. Do you think they're watching
us? Can they hear us?"

"No." He knew that because he knew every inch of this
compound. This was the room they put people in who were
never coming out alive. Whatever they had to say to their
captors or to each other was of no consequence to the
O'Rourkes now.

This was a room he'd prayed he'd never be in but counted
on being put in anyway. "Listen, under the tile in the left
corner…lift it. Use your nail or something."

She held up her short, clipped nails but then hurried over
to the corner and began to claw at the tile anyway.

She came back with a key.

"Nice job," he said.

"Who the hell are you?" she asked in return.

"I'm your only shot out of here."

"Funny, I thought that we were both each other's shot."

"Touché. Now, listen to me carefully," he explained, and
she waited, eyes locked on his. "When we go into the hall,
I'll disable the guard. They only keep one down here because
these cells are virtually indestructible. As soon as I do, grab
his chair and get up and rip the wires out of the camera. Can
you do that?"

"I'm not the one you should be worried about. You can't
even hold your head up straight," she pointed out. He grunted,
his pride aching along with most everything else, and he
pushed himself to his feet and toward the door.

Callie was right on his heels, her breathing sharp and fast,
the intensity of what they were about to do pulsing through

the air. Her breasts rubbed his back and for a second he put his forehead against the door, trying to get rid of the vertigo and just letting himself feel.

Callie felt really damn good. It had to be the concussion making him all soft and sweet and wanting to hug this woman who was saving his ass as much as he was saving hers.

Whether or not he could truly trust her remained to be seen, but it was the least of his concerns.

Key in the lock, he turned the knob inch by excruciating inch and eased the door open to get a glimpse of the guard. End of the hallway, back to the door, sitting half-asleep.

Leo had visited this area enough to know that the person who took the night shift guarding these doors had the cushiest job in the place.

He slid down the hall as his training clicked into place. With one careful, silent foot in front of the other, he made it safely along the corridor.

Adrenaline, pure and simple, pumped through him as he overpowered the guard. Callie had quietly and effectively blocked the camera at the same time, and within seconds Leo had the man's gun, knife, cash and ID.

"This way," he urged, and she followed him down another dark hallway. He used the guard's knife to slash through the trigger wires of the alarm before pushing out a side door that led into the deep woods of the O'Rourke estate. A place many had tried to escape from and into and never could.

Leo never went in without a plan. Someone at his office knew that. The same someone who, no doubt, had purposely blown his cover because honestly, his plan A was something.

But what the snitch didn't know was that he always counted on plans A, B and C failing.

He held Callie's hand tightly as he moved them toward plan D.

JUSTIN DIDN'T HAVE a lot of options. The threat to Turk's life could be a fake, but he doubted it. The fact that someone— anyone—had made the connection between Turk and Ava wasn't the best news. The fact that Ava was involved in something that could possibly end her career was second on the list to saving Turk, but none of it was good.

Ava was looking to him to do something. The problem was, that something was going to get all of them in deep trouble.

"I'll call someone I know in the DEA," he said finally as they sped along the highway.

Ava had remained silent for the past half hour, following all his directions as if on autopilot. But she'd stopped crying, at least, had let herself lose control for all of three minutes before she told him she was fine, wiped her eyes impatiently and stared straight ahead.

"A friend of Leo's?" she asked.

"Yes."

Justin and Cash had worked with Karen last year on a Gray Ops mission that Turk had set up for them because it involved Hawaii, surfing, and a chance to help out the DEA.

Working for an agency like that had a much longer shelf life than that of an active-duty SEAL, something Justin had to seriously consider if he wasn't planning to go the career-military route.

Karen was thirty. A top field agent. Gorgeous. They'd enjoyed each other's company in Hawaii but agreed it wasn't going any further.

Didn't mean he couldn't call in a favor.

"Did you date her?"

"No," he said, because that was the truth. And then he dialed the phone so he could end this line of questioning.

It was Karen's secured cell-phone line. She had his, too.

His name would flash on the screen along with two stars, which was code for, *I'm in trouble.*

"What's happened?" Karen asked, not bothering with hello, obviously recognizing Justin's emergency call.

"I've got Leo's sister with me," he started.

"The A.D.A."

"Yes." He repeated the caller's threat to Karen, saw Ava wince and turn away.

Karen was silent for a moment. "Does she know where Susie Mercer is?"

"No."

"You're sure."

"I'm sure, Karen."

"Why are you with Leo's sister? Did you have prior knowledge of this?" Karen asked, and Justin gritted his teeth and prepared to lie through them at the same time. No way was he getting Turk into even more trouble, no matter how cool Karen was.

"I was in New York visiting Ava."

"Convenient that you were there just at the time Ava received the threat about Leo."

"We're together. A couple," he said, ignoring the way Ava's body whipped around toward him.

"Since when?"

"A while now."

"Funny, Leo never mentioned that. Or you, a few months ago."

"It was more of a whirlwind thing. Will you keep me posted about Leo?"

"You know I can't do that, Justin. But you can keep me posted if you hear anything further. And you should turn the A.D.A. over to us. For safekeeping."

"She's safe with me."

"She's involved with our case and *you* are *not*. Bring her—"

He clicked the phone shut. "We got cut off," he said by way of explanation to Ava, who was still staring at him. Because the words *dating, whirlwind* and *his* weren't exactly in his everyday vocabulary.

Ava's cross-examination skills kicked into high gear. "She thinks we're dating?"

"Yes."

"You're not telling her about Leo's first call to you, then?"

"That's not a good idea."

"Can she help?"

"She's looking into it."

"What about Leo? Has she heard from him?"

He glanced over to her, wishing he had something better to tell her. "She's looking into that, too."

THE TRAFFIC WHIZZED by and Ava had to concentrate on looking straight ahead out the windshield. "Leo's supervisor's looking into it, but she couldn't confirm—" she started, then stopped before her voice broke more.

"Ava," Justin said, but she remained facing the window and wouldn't look at him. "Your brother's trained."

"So was my father, remember?" She hated the way her voice cracked with fear and grief and anger.

Sometimes the emotions hit her hard and unexpectedly. Although she'd spent her life trying to slam down the various doors that led to them, they kept popping up in front of her. Because she was a woman, because she was a little sister of an overprotective big brother and because she'd been in love with her brother's best friend for years.

That realization hit her like a giant punch in the stomach,

probably because it was the first time she'd actually allowed the full truth to break through her consciousness.

Ava was always much more comfortable around men, felt their mind-set better suited hers. They got her drive in a way few women did.

Or maybe she was lying to herself, since she knew the man who could handle her could also, and had, brought her so much heartache.

She didn't believe that teens didn't know what love was. No, she believed that teens had a clarity of the soul and that love was best suited to describe what some of them felt because their lives were usually far less complicated.

She'd convinced herself that she'd gotten over Justin as far as her heart was concerned, that it was just her body that was the problem. She knew better now.

"I don't want to get you in trouble," she began. "I don't want you to have to lie."

"I didn't lie…much," he said, glanced at her and gave her a smile that said, *I'm used to trouble.* "No one can prove I didn't come up to visit you on my own. No way for anyone to disprove it, either. That's good enough in my book."

"We need a better plan, Justin. For everything. If you're not going to let me do anything to help Leo, you've got to let me make sure you're not going to suffer the consequences, and that Leo won't get into more trouble."

"How's that going to happen? Once they realize that your brother called me first, we're both screwed."

"Not if you were there with me at the time for personal reasons—they can't prove otherwise. We can just stick to our story."

"You know the truth, I know the truth." He shook his head

and stared at the road ahead. The white lines whizzed by so fast that she felt dizzy and out of control. And angry. So very angry.

"You have no right to come back into my life after nine years, yank me from my home, my job, and then tell me that there's nothing I can do to help save my brother or my friend."

"What do you want from me, Ava? He's my best god-damned friend. Don't you think I'm worried, too? Don't you think I'd lay down my life for him? For you?"

"You owe me the truth," she said, her voice back to sounding firm and strong. "You're asking me to trust you—the way I used to. I'm having trouble doing that. I want us to get past what happened."

"We don't have time for old home week."

"That didn't matter to you back at the motel." She practically spat the words at him.

"Believe me, that didn't matter to you back there, either."

"You never even tried to get in touch with me."

"You didn't exactly come after me," he said, unable to keep the hurt out of his tone.

"I didn't know."

"Of course you knew. You and the entire freakin' town knew that Gina miscarried and that she found another guy. The worst part was that it didn't matter that Gina had hooked up with someone else. I didn't know what to do for her or for myself."

"Wasn't your family there for you?" Ava asked. "I mean, I know you and your parents didn't always see eye to eye, but they're still family."

"You have a hell of a lot of misconceptions about my family," he muttered.

"Your family would've done anything for you."

"You're in some very dangerous territory, Ava."

"Why can you know all of my family secrets, but I'm not allowed to know any of yours? Probably because there are none."

"You wouldn't have been able to handle my secrets, or my family's," he said in a tone that should've warned her to back off.

But she couldn't. It had been bottled up too long and there were too many unanswered questions between them. "Did you and Gina break up because she lost the baby?"

The tension Justin gave off was palpable. She wasn't sure he was even going to answer her, but finally, he did.

"I don't know if we'd still be together today if she hadn't lost the baby. But I stuck to my responsibilities. I stayed faithful to my vows. She didn't."

But he didn't look comfortable.

"It's okay if you're still in love with her. You'll probably always be in love with her."

"I'm not, all right? I didn't love her," he said, his voice raw now.

"I don't understand."

He wouldn't look at her, kept his attention on the road. "She didn't deserve what she got. She didn't love me, either."

"You guys didn't have to get married. I mean, there were other options…"

"I wasn't the father."

"What?"

"My brother was—my millionaire, three ex-wives and God knows how many mistresses by now, brother was the father. And when she told him about the baby, he laughed and threw a couple of hundreds at her, told her to take care of her own problem." Justin sounded as if he was being strangled, as if it killed him to talk about this.

But at least he was still talking.

"So what happened?"

"She refused. She went home, told her parents and they threw her out. I beat the shit out of my brother. And that's when everything hit the fan. Since I wasn't the golden boy, the one poised to run the family business and marry the proper woman anyway, my father threatened to have me arrested for assault if I didn't comply with his terms. And I sure as hell didn't want a criminal record—it would have ruined my military career before it'd even started."

"So you were forced to marry her?"

He nodded, his jaw tight. "She also had nowhere else to go, no one to turn to. I couldn't let that happen. I told everyone that the baby was mine, and took all the flak. Everyone in town believed it and I got cut off, but my father kept his end of the bargain and the cops didn't arrest me."

"They would've had no right to arrest you."

"I put him in the hospital. And then I got married. I enlisted to get a steady paycheck, moved out and Gina and I got a shitty apartment. I never even consummated the marriage. But I would've been a damn good father to that baby," he said fiercely.

"I know that." She touched his arm but he jerked it away, as if the gesture was too much.

"We'll be there in about an hour," he said. "I'd never forgive myself if anything happened to you, and I already have too many things I can't forgive myself for. I'm not going down with this one on my conscience."

"WE'RE GOING UNDERGROUND." Leo managed to speak the words through panting breaths. Callie was faring much better than he was, although he refused to admit that she'd been holding him up on their run through the dark woods.

"Underground?" she asked.

He reached into the pile of leaves before him until he felt

the handle. One good yank that nearly tore out his arm and made his head throb harder and in tandem with his heartbeat, and the trapdoor creaked open.

She peered down. "It's dark."

"It's safe." He put a hand on her lower back. "There's a ladder along this wall. Take it slowly. There's a flashlight at the bottom of the stairs. Don't turn it on until I shut the door."

She paused for a second, until she heard alarms begin to blare. Lights flashed and the sound of barking dogs seemed to come at them from all directions.

"Go now, Callie," he told her, and she did.

Minutes later, they were in pitch-darkness. Then Callie clicked on the flashlight and the thin beam of light helped him down the rest of the ladder to the safe ground she'd already found.

"What is this place?" she asked, touching the dirt walls then staring up at the low ceiling. Leo crouched down so his head wouldn't hit it.

"They used the hideout and tunnel in the 1920s, during Prohibition, to run their illegal liquor. No one's been down here in a long time. O'Rourke thinks it's been demolished."

"What's waiting for us at the other end?" she asked.

"Hopefully, freedom."

But before he could explain further, the flashlight dimmed and then went out completely.

"That's not good," she whispered.

"Scared of the dark, Callie?"

"No, it's not the dark that gets me. It's the small space. Walls closing in and all that." She tried a laugh but he could hear the real fear in her tone.

"Put your hands on me," he said. She reached out and made contact, clearly careful not to grab him too hard, even now.

He put one of his hands over hers, where she held him at his waist, and the other he kept extended to ward off walking into any walls. "Your eyes should adjust soon, it'll get easier."

Her figure pressed his again and his entire body reacted. Again.

Not the time or the place, Leo.

Sensitive parts of him let him know that they didn't care about his mind's cautionary warnings. "Is there anyone at home who's going to be looking for you?"

"No, there's not."

"Work?"

"Considering it was Friday night, not until Monday."

"No boyfriends?"

"No."

"Husband?"

"Is this an interrogation?"

"I'm just a naturally curious guy, Callie."

"What about you? Who's waiting for you?"

"There's no one at home," he admitted, wondered why it unexpectedly hurt to say that.

For him, there hadn't been anyone serious since high school, when Justin had stolen Leo's girlfriend *and* told him that Ava was hot all within the first five hours of their meeting. Leo had punched Justin square in the jaw and then pushed the bigger guy right down to the gym floor.

Back then, Justin had been well versed in the art of the brawl, but Leo had the advantage of his father's Delta and DEA training. Justin was immobilized in minutes.

Justin came over later that same day to apologize…and to ask Leo to show him those moves.

As Leo got more and more involved in his own DEA job, everything else, including the hope for a relationship, fell away. Single-minded, just like his father, he supposed. "Are you doing all right back there?" he asked.

"Keep talking. It helps when you talk. Tell me about yourself. Tell me a story—anything."

"I've got something for you. When we get out of this, I'll take you out someplace. I'd want you to dress up. I can picture you with your hair down, your feet bare…"

"No place is going to serve us in bare feet," she told him.

"I'm thinking of someplace private—an island, the beach—our own private dinner. Your dress swirling in the wind. You're laughing."

"And I'll know your name, finally? Or will I have to just keep calling you green eyes?"

Leo smiled. "I'll let you know once we get there."

8

AVA TRIED to imagine being eighteen and facing the world alone. Having no family or friends, ostracized, facing a threat of jail time and a baby on the way. Then married to someone without love, or possibly little more than pity, and a chill overtook her.

He'd been so alone, especially with Leo away at college when Justin first enlisted and went through boot camp.

She and Justin, both heartbroken.

She had no idea what to say to him. The story he'd told her was so different from what she'd imagined over the years. Leo had never let on, so she'd assumed that Justin and Gina had been happy but that the pain of losing the baby had torn them apart.

To know that Justin had never felt anything for Gina, that his family hadn't stuck up for him…that they'd all been so alone in their pain was nearly too much for her to handle.

"I wish I'd known," she said. "I wish I could have helped. Done something."

"It's over."

But it wasn't over for him. She could still hear the pain in his voice when he'd talked about it. "That part's over, yes. But the feelings—"

"I told you. There were no feelings between Gina and me."

"I don't mean between you and Gina. I mean, the feelings between you and me, Justin. Maybe they weren't strong enough… Maybe that's why you didn't come to me for help."

"You're trying to make sense out of a senseless situation," he told her.

How could she say that's what she did best? "If you had to do it all over again…" she started to ask, even though she didn't want to know the answer. Even though she already knew what it would be.

"I don't second-guess myself. I'd have done the same thing, Ava."

WOULD THE UTTER and complete humiliation never stop? It was made worse as Ava watched him with a look that had too much sorrow in it for Justin's comfort.

It's time to act like a man. His father's words bounced between his ears until he wanted to scream. The horrible night when his life's plan had been irrevocably altered was stuck in the forefront of his mind.

Justin and his brother, James, were fraternal twins, Justin being older by three minutes. Light to James's dark, that was only the beginning of a long line of differences guaranteed to make sure the brothers were never really friends.

His brother had laughed—laughed, when Justin had tried to talk to him about Gina being pregnant.

"You have to help her," he'd said.

"I don't have to do anything…she was stupid enough to get pregnant. That's not my fault." James had stared him down.

"She said you told her that you loved her."

"I tell all of them that. That's what women want to hear, Justin. That's all it takes to get them into bed," James had said, sounding so much like their father.

At his brother's words, the rage had built inside of Justin to an almost unbearable level.

The fight had been brutal. And Justin had had to restrain himself from using some of the moves he'd learned from Turk and Turk's dad. Moves that Turk's dad had told him made Justin's hands deadly weapons, which was not a responsibility to be taken lightly.

He could barely see straight during most of the time he and James had slammed around the floor. He still wasn't sure who called the police because his parents hadn't been home at the time. It could have been the housekeeper or even one of the neighbors.

The police were already there when the ambulances arrived. Next, it was the E.R. James had suffered a concussion, as well as bruises and contusions. Justin had broken his left hand, which still ached to this day when it rained. It was a persistent reminder of the day everything in his life had gone sickeningly downhill.

His hand still throbbed as he was married a week later. He'd felt worse. The deal, made behind an E.R. curtain, had made him so sick to his stomach that he'd thrown up all over the doctor.

Marry Gina so she wouldn't spread a rumor that James, the perfect son, had gotten her pregnant. Take responsibility for the baby or get charged with assault and battery. Justin had planned on enlisting in the navy and getting his degree with the military's help rather than take money from his parents anyway. But any kind of criminal record would haunt him, and make becoming an officer next to impossible.

He'd been so young, so scared and cornered. Turk's father had died months earlier, the only man who, at that point, might've been able to help Justin out of the situation. The man whose influence gave Justin the moral code he'd needed to make something of himself, instead of continuing along the bad-boy rebel path that was getting him nowhere.

Water under the bridge.

Gina had sobbed through their lonely, rushed ceremony. Come to think of it, Justin probably would've sobbed too, if not for the fact that Gina's father held a gun to his back. Literally. He'd shown him the pistol hidden in his suit jacket right before the ceremony began.

He'd never felt more alone than he had on that day—no family to support him, Turk already back at school and Ava gone for her first year of college and no longer speaking to him. Turk would've been there for him, but Justin didn't tell him anything until weeks later. They'd had their own fight about it and hadn't spoken for over four months, until that horrible day when Gina went for an exam and the doctor discovered that the baby was no longer moving.

Turk had caught the red-eye, found Justin sitting in a park near his apartment building with his head in his hands and his world once again spinning out of control.

"I just want to be in control—in charge of my own life, not just following it along," he remembered telling his friend.

"Then take it back. Now," Turk told him. It had taken Justin another few months, but eventually the divorce proceedings were in place and he'd entered BUD/S in his bid to become a SEAL. At that point, he'd wanted the most bone-crunching, emotionally tiring experience he could get, wanted everything wrung out of him bit by bit.

Becoming a SEAL had been like being rebuilt from the ground up. His instructor at the time told him that he had everything it took to become a SEAL. He just needed to believe it, and in himself. And finally, he had—made it through Hell

Week and been secured with twelve others, down from a class that started with over a hundred and twenty men. Control had been hard won, but it had been worth it. And it was all his.

A firm grasp on his wrist shook him back to reality. And no, this wasn't the old courthouse in Norfolk. He was headed for his home, with Ava, and his future was uncertain. Again.

But Ava's fingers were cool against his skin, calming, almost. Grounding. And if he stared into her eyes long enough, he could almost believe that this could be real, the way Turk had told him all those years ago…

"What's up?" Justin asked as soon as he slammed the passenger-side door shut. It was a little after two in the morning, which didn't bother Justin as much as being forced to climb out of his warm bed and come out in the freezing cold of another crappy Virginia winter.

Turk put his foot heavily on the gas and shot the old Buick down the stretch of icy, deserted highway. "It's about Ava."

"When is it not?" Justin asked as Turk took a curve at high speed. Justin finally noticed his friend's tense posture. "Look, is she all right? Did someone hurt her?"

"She thinks she loves you."

Justin stared at Turk's profile, unable to speak for a moment. "She told you that?"

"She didn't have to tell me. I just know."

"Last I checked, you weren't an expert on women and their feelings."

"My sister's in love with you. I don't know how I didn't notice it until yesterday." Turk shook his head as he pulled the car, with its now overheating engine, off to the side of the highway. Turk cursed and let himself out of the car, Justin following at his heels.

"You're wrong," Justin insisted as Turk opened the hood

and steam billowed into the freezing air. Justin shoved his hands into his pockets—he'd forgotten gloves in his haste to meet up with his friend, and he hoped there was a blanket in this car as well.

"Not about this. Grab the water and antifreeze from the trunk, will you."

"Turk, she doesn't love me. She doesn't even know what love is," *he called out as he opened the battered trunk and hauled out the two bottles. He handed the antifreeze to Turk and held on to the water.*

"Yeah, you say that to her so you can sound like every single adult asshole we've ever met." *Turk stared at him.* "She's got it bad for you. I could tell by the way she was watching you tell that stupid story last night about the time you pulled the fire alarm at your old boarding school to get out of your suspension."

"How exactly was she looking at me?"

"Like your stupid story was interesting. Like you were some superhero." *Turk paused.* "I'm not pissed at you. I know you wouldn't take advantage of her or hurt her. Not intentionally."

Justin shuffled his feet in the snow. White flakes had started to come down hard as Turk went underneath the hood. "She's just got a crush," *he said to Turk's back.*

"Whatever it is, she's got it bad."

"It'll pass."

Turk came out from under the hood and paused for a long second while staring at Justin. "She's going out with the quarterback this weekend, you know."

Justin didn't say anything, instead he gripped the bottle of water so tightly that the plastic crumpled in his hand.

Turk chuckled softly. "As long as you feel the same way, I guess it's all right."

Justin hadn't bothered to argue then, either.

"The DEA wants me to turn you in to them. For protection. Karen will be waiting for you at the safe house," he told Ava now, barely able to speak over the lump in his throat.

She shook her head, nearly imperceptibly. But he saw it, got it. It was all he needed to make him jerk the wheel, stopping the car along the side of the road.

"There's someplace else we could go," he said. "A place the team and I use that we keep secret." Even though Rev had secured Justin's own house earlier, once the DEA got involved that was no longer an option—his own house was obviously the first place they'd look. He'd originally picked that location because he'd have the home turf advantage—because he'd have Rev and Cash and his other teammates close by for support. Now, he wasn't going to get them tangled up in all of this. Besides, the cabin was far more high tech than his own house could ever be.

"Go there," she said.

"You've got to think this through—"

"I'm not going into protective custody. Leo will take care of what he needs to. In the meantime, I'm staying with you."

He didn't ask her again as he prepared to break every freakin' rule in the book and rewrite them his own way.

He knew Ava all too well, knew himself, too. One night wasn't too much to ask. One night and he'd make sure that she was placed where she should be. She'd hate him for it, no doubt, but in order to keep her safe he was going to have to let her go.

"It'll be okay," she offered.

He nodded, not believing that at all. "We'll be there soon."

"Yesterday I was getting ready for the biggest case of my career."

A little while ago, you were in my arms…

"I know," he said quietly, and this time he dropped one hand off the steering wheel.

She held on to it tightly.

LEO AND CALLIE ended up at an all-night gas station and rest stop that was nearly deserted, save for a lone man behind the counter and a few weary truckers.

He wasn't sure anymore whom he could trust in the DEA, but he did know there was always one person in the entire world he could trust with his life. Hands down, no questions asked.

He put the change into the pay phone and dialed. When the phone on the other end rang once, he put the receiver back in the cradle. Then he dialed the same number again, let the phone ring three times before hanging up. An old signal, but one that Justin would recognize.

Now it was time to put some more distance between him and the O'Rourke gang.

"See that old Chevy?" He didn't point, motioned with a small tilt of his head that almost made him fall over in pain.

"Yes."

"Just walk over to the passenger's side, like you're waiting for me to open the door."

"You're not going to be able to drive," she told him. "How about you walk over to the passenger's side?"

"Because I'm the one who needs to start the car, unless you've got keys to it I don't know about," he said, but she'd already started walking toward the car, obviously opting for her own plan.

The doors were unlocked, which was the reason he'd picked that particular car in the first place. She was already in the driver's seat, the panel below the steering wheel yanked out and wires exposed by the time he'd gotten in himself.

Within seconds, the engine rolled over. She didn't bother to replace the panel, instead, just pulled out of the parking lot as if she was in no hurry at all.

Once they got onto the highway, she gunned it.

"What the hell did you do before you became a social worker?" he asked.

Callie didn't answer him. His thoughts were spinning and he heard himself pulling hard for a breath. Still, he grabbed for the gun and held it on her.

"You're going to shoot the only chance we've got of getting out of all of this?" she asked calmly.

"You're cool under pressure. You know your way around injuries. You can hot-wire a car. Did you pick all of this up from your street kid clients, Callie?"

"Maybe." She stared at him with a look in her eyes similar to that of a caged lion's.

He didn't doubt that some major self-defense moves came in this pretty, defiant package, as well. "What you're *not* telling me could get us both killed."

"You can hot-wire a car, too," she started. "You worked for the O'Rourke family. You handle a gun, you almost killed a man in front of me. And you're obviously wanted. So, you first. Because I don't even know your name."

He opened his mouth to tell her that he wasn't satisfied with her answer, that none of this was a joke, that she was in a lot of danger, but the adrenaline that had gotten him this far suddenly disappeared.

He was vaguely aware of Callie calling his name, touching his cheek and his chest, slipping the gun from his hand, but *dammit,* he didn't care about anything except the heaviness that overtook him.

9

Ava dozed for most of the two-hour drive to the cabin. She'd reclined the seat at Justin's suggestion and exhaustion overtook her. When she woke, she found herself staring up at him, her head resting on her arm.

She could barely make out his profile—stoic, staring straight ahead—but she didn't doubt for a second that he knew she was awake.

"Good timing," he said after a few seconds. "We're here."

She pushed the seat upright and stared out at the dark cabin he'd parked next to. It looked solidly built, a one-floor job with a large, wraparound porch covering three sides. "What is this place?"

"A couple of my teammates and I built it a few years back. The land belongs to our CO. It's kind of an experiment."

"An experiment?" she asked sleepily.

"It's a prototype, actually." He stared up at the nondescript cabin. "Rev is using this place to develop the ultimate in high-tech security."

"So this has nothing to do with your SEAL work, then?"

"No. It's about preparing for the future," he said. "Come on, let's get settled inside."

He opened his door and grabbed his bag from the back seat. She followed suit in her bare feet and caught up with him on the porch. "Your team's going to worry about you soon, aren't they?"

"I'm on leave, but yeah. They'll start wondering soon."

"Probably worried enough to come looking for you."

"We've still got a while before that would happen. I won't be UA for another six days." He punched some numbers into a small black device attached to a ring of keys he'd pulled from his pocket, and she watched in amazement as the heavy door slid open.

"It's solid steel," he explained as he motioned her into the cabin. The door closed quietly behind them with a solid *thunk*. Justin punched in some more buttons to the device. "We're okay for now."

The main room was furnished casually, with a couple of beige couches that looked comfortable enough, a few bookcases and a TV, and the kitchen was toward the back of the cabin.

There were also lots of windows.

"They're tinted," he said when he saw her looking. "You can see out, no one can see in. They're also bulletproof."

"Good. That's…good."

"I know you're worried about Leo and Callie, but the best thing we can do for him now is to keep you safe. Out of harm's way. That's what he asked me to do and that's what I'm going to do."

"Whether I like it or not, right?"

"Right," he agreed sincerely, and that got a small snort from her.

She sighed. "It's just that…I could be doing something. Maybe we can figure out where Leo's being held—"

"If he's being held."

"They know he's my brother. They know who he is."

"Not necessarily. His cover could've included an A.D.A.

sister named Ava. Sometimes, when you're telling a lie, you have to have a lot of the truth in there to pull it off."

Still, she wasn't all that satisfied. "There's got to be something we can do."

"If there is, we'll do it," he promised. "Let me show you around here some more."

He explained the alarm system, the secret basement bunker that was filled with cameras and its own bedroom and bathroom. And weapons. He told her, "If anyone comes, go down here and lock yourself in. Don't wait for me if I'm not around."

She didn't bother to protest. His eyes held that dangerous glitter that let her know it was better not to argue.

This place, with its high-tech security, was unbelievable. "Is all of this expensive?"

"As a whole, it would be marketed to wealthy clientele. But bits and pieces could easily be adapted by just about anyone."

She thought about the peace of mind some of this equipment could bring women who lived life looking over their shoulder and her stomach clenched with fear. *Callie.*

"I need to make a call."

Justin shook his head. "Not now. Not for a while."

"It's a really important call."

"Ava—" He ran a hand through his hair. "I'll make it for you."

"You can't. She won't accept a call from you. Only from me, from my number. And I barely have any charge left."

"You're being impossible. Don't you realize that anyone you call…"

"Anyone I call could be my enemy? Could turn me in to the O'Rourkes?" She marched to grab her cell phone and flipped it open, daring him to stop her.

He didn't. Instead he crossed his arms and watched her as Callie's message began to play. She forced herself to stare at

Justin in that defiant way he'd expect. And then she closed the phone without leaving a message.

"Why are you shaking?" he asked, his drawl thickening, the way it did when he was angry. "Don't play games with me now. Tell me everything you know."

"It's nothing that could help the DEA find Leo. Callie is a social worker who was on the Susie Mercer case—she's also my good friend. I met her last year when I started doing some volunteer work for her."

He narrowed his eyes. "What kind of work?"

"Helping abused women."

"Like Susie Mercer."

"Yes."

"How?"

She shifted from foot to foot under the interrogation in a way she never did with anyone. "I can't tell you that."

He took a step forward, stood less than an inch from her. "You have to tell me. You will tell me."

"Don't push me, Justin."

"What? The way you didn't push me in the car? The way you didn't force me to spill my deepest secrets to you? The ones that won't help to save your brother's life."

"I don't know where Susie is! Neither does Callie." She shoved him hard against the chest. He, of course, didn't move an inch, but rather grabbed her arms and held her easily. Gently. More gently than she would've expected.

"Let me in, Ava. Maybe we can piece all of this together."

"Callie helps abused women leave their husbands," she started. "If a woman's husband doesn't get convicted, or she's too scared to press charges but still wants to leave, Callie helps them disappear. A kind of witness protection program, run for women, by women."

"Who funds it?"

"It doesn't take much, really. You'd be surprised how many people are willing to help. It's an entire network of people throughout the country…a lot of them are the women we've helped. It's all done anonymously."

"So Callie really doesn't know where Susie is?"

She shook her head. "There are only two people at all times who follow the chain. Susie's gone through the system and she's free. On her own. Neither of us know now…only the last woman in the chain typically knows the whereabouts of the woman who's escaping, and this time, even that last woman doesn't know. Couldn't know. Susie refused to put anyone in more danger than necessary. She's so brave, Justin."

"So the men who are after Susie don't know anything about your system?"

"I don't think so. I think they're just using Callie and me as the last-known links to Susie."

"So how the hell did they figure out who Leo is?" he asked, letting go of her so he could walk a short distance, trying to problem solve the situation. He stopped, stared at the wall. "Does Callie know what your brother does for a living?"

"Yes. But she didn't know what case he was working on. Even I didn't know that."

He turned. "You have pictures of Leo. In your house."

"Yes. Of course."

He nodded. "That's how they must have made the connection, since they were following you and Callie, looking for clues on Susie."

"I really did blow his cover."

"Maybe. But it wasn't on purpose. Just a case of really, really bad luck. Still, you should have told me this. All of this."

"I'm not supposed to tell anyone about what Callie does."

"And I'm not just anyone," he told her, his face a cross between hurt and anger right before his phone beeped to distract him.

She saw him take it out of his pocket and stare hard at the number instead of answering.

It was the same thing he'd done twice on the ride to the cabin. She'd heard the phone ring in her sleep, opened her eyes briefly, then watched him watch the number and wait for the phone to stop ringing.

All three times, it stopped after three rings.

"Your phone—why does it keep doing that?" she asked.

He stared at the screen quickly, then shut it. "Yeah, it's just a wrong number."

"I don't believe you."

"Right now I don't really care what you believe. I'm going to shore things up outside and hide the car. Stay in here and stay off the phone," he ordered. The door slid open, then closed and she heard the click of the locks. He'd most definitely locked her inside. She picked up the bowl from a table nearby and was prepared to throw it at the door. Ava imagined it breaking with a satisfying crack.

She realized that would solve nothing, placed it back down on the table and took some deep breaths.

Her father always said that you got angriest at the people you love the most—those you knew who wouldn't run away from a fight.

Justin left the cabin, but he wasn't running, not away from her. He'd run away with her. And as angry as they were with each other, the deeper feelings were there. Undeniably there. Whether he'd admit them was another story. And in those moments, watching the door, she decided that she needed to try to get through to him.

AFTER A NICE warm shower, something that would forever remind her of Justin, Ava changed into a U.S. Navy T-shirt and shorts and went back to the kitchen, her hair still wet and dripping. Justin was nowhere in sight, but she felt his presence as surely as if he was next to her. His presence and his anger.

She padded toward the kitchen. Finding it well stocked, she opened some soup and heated it while she rummaged for crackers. Justin was muttering to himself as he came in the door.

She turned to see him soaked with mud on the entire right side of his body, and cursing up a storm. "What happened?"

"Rev must've set up some kind of backwater Cajun trap off the side porch," he said. "Going to kill him next time I see him." He stripped the wet T-shirt off and it hit the floor with a *thwack,* splashing dirt everywhere.

"Hey, give me that. I'll wash it out," she said.

"I can wash it out myself." He worked the button and zipper on his jeans, apparently forgetting what he was doing until he was standing completely naked in front of her.

For a second, they just stared at each other.

"Your soup's overflowing," he said finally.

She heard the hissing behind her, but couldn't take her gaze from the way the light bounced off his hard chest, shadowed his rippled abs, as well as the cut of muscle above his hipbone that she'd earlier longed to trace with her finger. She had the sudden urge to do many things again as the ache between her legs intensified.

He was still angry, but his expression softened slightly. Maybe it was how she'd looked at him, or maybe it was because he did understand, more than she thought. "It's Leo who's calling me."

"Oh my God, how do you know? Why does he hang up?"

"He's making his way to safety…he's giving me his trail.

Please don't make me tell you things you're going to have to answer questions about later. I haven't spoken with him. I don't know if he's alone. I don't know about Callie. I don't know anything."

"So, it looks like we've both been holding things back," she said as she walked toward him. He stood his own ground, but his jaw clenched and he swallowed hard. The mud wasn't going to deter her. "You're nervous, aren't you? I make you nervous."

"Do not."

She brushed a hand down his bare chest, felt him actually start at her touch. She stopped her exploration when her hand hit the light trail of hair that led down between his legs and thickened around his cock. "It's going to be all right."

"I'm supposed to be the one telling you that."

She leaned forward and pressed a kiss to his shoulder, let her lips open slightly to lick a small path along his skin. A visible shudder ran through his body, and the start of a groan escaped his lips. She could tell he was trying hard not to give in.

"I don't want to think about the real reason we're here," she said, murmuring to his chest. "I'm tired of thinking. I just want to feel. Can you help me with that?"

The wall between them—the years of misunderstanding and separation and frustration—had just been leveled to the ground. And she would not give Justin the chance to rebuild it. She'd claw her way over the rubble, with bare feet and hands, first.

She would tear him down, too, touch by touch, rid him of any further resistance. Her fingers slid down lower still and he continued to protest by keeping his hands fisted at his sides. "You know all about bombs and weapons, but do you know what to do with me?"

"I know exactly what to do with you, Ava. You just trust me on that."

In that space nothing mattered but the way Justin watched her, alert, totally attentive, his brown eyes rapt to hers even as he struggled to stay in control.

Hard to do when he was completely naked and so obviously not in control at all. She figured it was time to even the playing field.

One small step back, away from him, and her shirt came off and floated to the floor with a soft *whoosh*. The cool air hit her skin and her nipples tightened as he sucked in a breath and just stared.

Her palms slid downward, to the waistband of the shorts. She wasn't good at slow. Tension vibrated the air between them, and the sound of her heart beating seemed to echo in the quiet of the room.

She'd never taken quite so much time undressing in her whole life. It was excruciating. But the look on his face as she shifted her hips to push the gray cotton down her thighs, the way his eyelids grew heavy, the slight flare of his nostrils, the way his lips parted slightly, was worth it.

He'd unconsciously pushed the tip of his tongue in between his teeth, his shoulders straightened, and his eyes…well, those had always told her everything she'd needed to know.

She wanted to hear him say her name in that infuriatingly sexy voice that got sexier whenever he was tired or drunk, or obviously turned on.

She'd discovered that last one back in high school. But now she wasn't seventeen and he wasn't going anywhere this time.

"Come here, Ava," he said finally. His voice sounded rough, taut, almost, but still full of command. And that was one order she was more than willing to follow.

10

JUSTIN'S VOICE sounded rough, husky, and his breath caught as Ava did exactly as he asked and pressed her naked body against his.

He'd lost any semblance of control when it came to her. The roar between his ears grew louder and as much as he'd miss the contact of her soft breasts rubbing his chest, he wished he could have stood there a while longer to just *look* at her. So damn pretty she broke his heart, the way her memory had done to him nearly every day since he'd met her.

His heart still hurt, mainly because it was halfway between healing and breaking apart fully, and he wasn't sure he'd be able to piece it back together after this happened. But he wasn't going to be able to stop, either.

He grabbed her around the waist, carried her to the couch and waited for her to protest, to push back, to argue, waited for the phone to ring or the earth to crumble or something, anything to postpone this the way the universe seemed to always want to.

When she did none of those things and the earth stayed on its axis, he almost backed off. Almost. But something in her eyes still held the hint of dare, asked for proof of something from him he wasn't sure he knew how to give. And yet he couldn't—wouldn't—back away now.

He laid her down on the couch, supported most of his weight on his arms so he could watch her. Still, her legs twined around his as if to hold him there.

"What do you want from me?" he murmured, then brushed a kiss over her lips. She tried, unsuccessfully, to swallow a moan, but that was her only answer. Her arms rested above her head, leaving her so open to him. So trusting.

Yeah, that was it. *Trust.* That's what she wanted and it was proving to be the hardest thing for both of them to give. She'd gotten closer than anyone ever had, but whether he would let her all the way in was yet to be seen.

His head dipped to catch a nipple in his mouth. He rolled it around his tongue until the peak was stiff and hot.

"Feels good…so good," she murmured.

And they were both wet and muddy against the cushions and he didn't care. Neither did Ava because she was tugging at him, murmuring for him to hurry, *to take her,* and she wasn't having to beg for much longer.

HEAT SIMMERED between her legs when Justin's mouth covered a nipple. She jerked toward him at the warm, wet contact of his tongue on the stiff peak, unable to stop her body from reacting.

His eyes were closed, as if all his concentration was focused on her breast.

She wanted so much more. "Justin, please…"

She clutched at his hair, his shoulders, but he shook his head, blew softly on her wet nipple. She closed her eyes and groaned in frustration.

"I'm not rushing through this," he said, his mouth closing in on her other nipple, holding it between his teeth while his tongue ruthlessly swiped the tip until she was grabbing at him, looking for any kind of balance.

She wanted his hands to join in the fun, wanted his large palms covering every part of her.

Slowly, *so slowly,* one of his hands traveled between her thighs to stroke her sex. His suckling her nipple intensified as she bucked, searching for any kind of relief.

The first time—and all other times without Justin would forever pale in comparison—with his slow, easy style forced her from simmer to a burn in seconds flat.

She melted, being completely and utterly at his mercy as he slipped a long finger inside of her, teased her, as the walls of her sex clenched. She rocked back and forth for a few minutes, but then he stopped.

Ava opened her mouth to protest, but he caught her clit with his thumb, pressed it until her breath hitched and she was almost gone.

His fingers strummed her and she stiffened, grabbed his arm so he couldn't pull away.

"Go ahead, Ava," he said in that maddening way he had. Even now, he acted as if he was in control of her—and her orgasm.

And *oh,* he certainly was. Her orgasm washed over her, made her a trembling mass of nerves as her belly tightened and her sex contracted around his fingers.

She didn't want to think about how he was making her feel, afraid if she did, it would all turn out to be a dream. So with her eyes shut tight she pictured Justin above her.

He was inside of her in one stroke, inside of her so deeply her womb ached with pleasure.

Something rumbled deep in his chest and she forced her eyes open. She saw the strain in his arms, his neck, holding back as if he wanted this to last forever.

His stomach muscles rippled under her opened palms and his eyes glowed, a dark, rich brown.

Eyes that seemed to see right through her at any given moment, and most especially at this moment.

Her arms tightened around his back as he pushed deeper and deeper, until her vision blurred and her nails scratched his skin.

Head buried against her neck, the old couch creaking underneath them, he took her for his own, bringing everything full circle.

11

THE GREEN-EYED MAN was still not waking up. Callie had made contact with the safe house four hours into the drive from Pittsburgh, and he'd barely stirred. She tried poking him every now and again.

At least he stirs. And cursed at her under his breath a little too, which was a good sign.

She'd stopped only once, pulling money out of his pants pocket for gas and to make a phone call. She pushed away the flood of memories that came down on her like a hard rain.

Yes, she'd been here before—done all of this too many times to count. It was like a homecoming she never, ever looked forward to.

And now, she also knew she wouldn't be returning to New York anytime soon.

Serena was waiting at the front porch. Her car was hidden somewhere along the road—her only reason for being here to let Callie into the safe house.

"I'll need some help bringing him inside," she told the older woman after they'd exchanged a rib-breaking hug.

They'd met ten years earlier when Callie had been in the early stage of her career as a social worker and felt overwhelmed by how little she could do to help anyone within her job's capacity.

Serena had come to her when she found herself faced with
a woman who wanted to leave her boyfriend of five years
again. He'd found her the first time, and the results Callie saw
in the case file had literally made her lose her lunch. Experi-
encing the boyfriend in person, threatening everyone in the
office, had made her angry. What made her storm out of the
place was the police telling her there wasn't much she could
do except fill out a report.

You can't do anything more until he actually touches you.

Serena didn't look much different than she did now, in jeans,
paint-splattered work shirt and long gray braid. She'd been
sitting on a bench outside Callie's office waiting for her.
Waiting to introduce her to the chain of women and the secret
method of helping them start over. And then she told her that
Callie's mom had been the beneficiary of such an organization.

"That's how you found me?" Callie had asked her.

"We've got to keep an eye on our own." Serena had winked
and Callie had known that everything was going to be okay.

Now Serena was peering into the car, one eyebrow cocked.

"It's not what you think. None of this is what you think."

"You know the rules. Don't ask, don't tell." Serena stared
at the sleeping man. "Can he walk at all? Because he looks
to be at least two-twenty."

Callie leaned in the car. "Hey, can you wake up a little? I
need your help."

"You don't know his name?" Serena asked, and then held
up her hand and shook her head.

Gradually, he stirred, his deep green eyes more familiar to
her than they should have been after knowing him for less than
twelve hours. "What the hell?"

"Come on, you're safe, you're fine. You just need to rest."

He seemed to remember that he wasn't all that happy with

her before he'd gone to sleep. He'd be less so once he fully understood that she'd brought him along on her ride, rather than wait for him to lead the way to safety.

He braced his weight on his arms and pushed himself up with what seemed like a Herculean force, and then he wobbled. He leaned on her and Serena heavily, but together they managed to get him inside and onto the double bed in the back room. He collapsed on the mattress, curled to one side and closed his eyes.

Callie left him to walk Serena to the door.

"How long?" Serena asked.

"Maybe a couple of days. I'm not really sure," Callie admitted.

"You know the drill." Serena gave her one last hug before disappearing into the night. Grateful for the lack of questions, mainly because she had too many of her own spinning around in her brain, Callie shut and locked the door quickly, secured the safety bolt and double-checked all the windows. Force of habit.

Then she brought some supplies to his bedside and proceeded to take care of him. A man she barely knew. A man with dangerous friends, and now, even more dangerous enemies.

He might have been one of them at one time, but he'd been held, same as her. And he'd saved her life.

He's going to want to know things...he's going to want to know everything. And for the first time, she realized that she wouldn't have any defenses. His weapons weren't physical, the kind that she could void with self-defense moves or a call to authorities or a cross-country move. No, his weapons were the way his body felt under her touch when she was scared shitless in the underground tunnel. The way he'd rescued her when she'd never ever let anyone do that for her.

The way he said her name, as if he was making love to her in his mind every time he did so, despite the pain and the danger.

She refused to think about that stupid prince-will-come song now. She had a job to do.

They'd both be gone soon enough, anyway.

Gingerly, she peeled off his T-shirt. They'd have nothing big enough to fit him here, so she'd wash it and his jeans tonight. Underwear too. Which meant she'd have to strip him.

A purely professional move.

She tugged at his jeans, slid them off and stared at his beautiful body for a few minutes. Her eyes lingered on his hard chest and abs.

He was strong and capable and kind, like few of the men she normally met in her line of work. And she let herself wonder, for just a few seconds, what it would be like to lie down next to him, to let him strip off her clothes and touch her until she was nothing but a body of quivering nerves.

She put a soft ice pack wrapped in a towel on his eye and cheek, timed twenty minutes while she cleaned off the other contusions on his body. This man had actively fought back, and hard, judging by the marks on his knuckles. These were not defensive wounds.

She realized she knew far too many medical terms, and far too few words to describe emotions like love.

When she turned off the lights and laid his gun and knife by the side of the bed, she curled up to his naked form and held him the way she wanted to be held.

It might have been minutes or possibly hours later when Ava floated back down to earth. Her insides were still fluttering from the intensity of her orgasm. She was covered in dried mud, and Justin's body was heavy on hers.

"Want to shower?" she asked from underneath him. He lifted his head from where it had been resting on her chest.

"Why? You want to spy on me again?" he teased.

Back then, he'd already been six foot three of solid muscle. Not as filled out as he was now, but enough to make her suck in her breath, even when she spotted him through the glass. Now he was perfect; muscles standing out in stark contrast to one another, shadowed planes and scars that she was sure hadn't been there before.

"I'd like to be in there with you this time," she said, and yes, she loved the way his smile took over his whole face. It was part mischievous but somehow all desire.

She buried her face in his neck as he carried her from the couch straight into the shower. He turned the water on and put them under once it warmed, let it drench them both at first.

He kissed her for a long time as the steam built, slowly, as if savoring every single taste of her. Their bodies slid together in a maddening grind until she didn't think she could stand it anymore, until her sex was aching and ready for him again.

He pressed her back against the shower tiles as the steam enveloped them. She whispered his name and smiled and he moved his hand between her legs.

"Love it when you moan," he whispered, his voice low and rough, which made her moan again.

"Love it when you do that."

The water was warm…soothing down her back. Safely in Justin's arms, her legs still wrapped around his waist, well, she wasn't planning on letting go. But he wasn't pushing inside her, not even when she tried to guide him.

"No, not yet. You're probably sore." He eased her down until her feet touched the tile floor and then he knelt between her legs.

He eased her thighs open, moved his head forward to kiss

the curls at the juncture between her thighs. She groaned as his tongue lapped her swollen, tender sex, his thumb relentless on her clit. She pressed herself to his mouth wantonly.

Her hands brushed the hard muscles along his shoulders as a tight, shivery sensation slid up her body and back down again. She forgot everything—everything—but the feel of his touch, probing her hot recesses.

One hand was on the soap dish to steady herself, the other on Justin's head to keep him where he was until blasts of pleasure tightened her belly and made her cries echo in the small bathroom.

THEY MADE IT to the bed after the water ran cool. Still wrapped in towels, she lay on top of the quilt next to Justin, feeling satiated. Her fingers traced the ridge of his bicep and for a few minutes more she was determined to pretend that everything was normal.

"You all right?" he asked. He'd been playing with her hair, running his fingers through the strands as it dried.

"Yes."

"Did you get that out of your system?" he asked.

"It was definitely more fun being with you in the shower than just watching," she said.

"More fun for me, too."

"Did you ever spy on me?"

"Never in the shower. You always locked the door. But one thing does stick out…you in the backyard in that rainbow-striped bikini during your senior year. Right before you stole my bike. Again."

She smiled at the memory. "You had the police pick me up."

"Well, yeah. It was the only way to teach you a lesson."

"Do you still have that bike?"

"Yes. Do you still have that bikini?"

"No."

"I guess naked will have to do."

"That's good, because we're running out of clothes," she murmured against the damp hair of his neck.

"We don't usually come up here to do laundry."

"I expect not. I'll wash them out."

"You don't have to take care of me like that."

"Maybe I want to. Maybe I like the idea of taking care of you for once."

"You used to take care of me all the time."

She lifted her head and brushed her hair out of his eyes. "What are you talking about?"

"When I used to sneak through your window."

"I thought that was because you told your parents you were staying with my brother."

"I didn't want to go home," he said. "Did you ever wonder why I'd stay on your floor instead of your brother's? Or the couch?"

Time after time, Justin would come in through her window. Sometimes it was early evening, sometimes well after midnight. Sometimes they talked until morning and sometimes they didn't talk at all.

"No. I guess I just liked having you close too much to question it." Her voice went soft with the memory of it. "In the morning, the pillow would smell like you."

She'd said that last part without thinking, but Justin didn't seem to mind. If anything, he tightened his grip around her a bit.

She hadn't really thought, after all this time, that they'd still have much in common. That they'd still be the same people they once were, that time, new jobs and life's hardships would have made them unrecognizable to one another.

She'd never expected that same, instant connection. That same longing.

He was different, but his core hadn't changed. He was still loyal, honest, a good man.

And yet she hadn't told him everything. "Where do we go from here, Justin?" she whispered. She'd thought he'd drifted off to sleep, hadn't expected his low, rough drawl.

"We go forward, Ava."

As if it was that simple. *We go forward...*

When she knew she couldn't stop herself from looking back.

12

A SHORT WHILE LATER, Justin woke up with a start and cursed himself for sleeping so soundly. He'd alarmed the place to within an inch of his life but still, this wasn't the time for snoozing. It probably wasn't the time to be making love to Ava either, but he was done with regrets in that area of his life.

He had a feeling, however, that Ava wasn't. Mainly because she'd managed to sneak away from under his arm and leave the bedroom. He threw on clothes as he walked through the cabin, found her in the kitchen soaking the burnt soup pan and searching the cabinets, looking as if she'd just woken up as well.

She pulled out more soup and some bread and busied herself while he sat at the table and watched her. Only asking if he was as hungry as she was and yeah, she wasn't ready to talk about what happened now that the first blush had worn off.

That was all right. It's not as if this was a relaxing situation. This entire situation was fraught with stress.

Sex was so much easier than talking. He debated the merits of seducing her again, right on the kitchen table, making everything right for a few more minutes…

"You're muttering to yourself," Ava told him as she put the plates down and sat across from him at the small table.

"Sorry. Nothing important." He was starving. And for a few minutes they bonded in the silence as they filled their stomachs.

"Leo told me that you made lieutenant," she said after she pushed her plate away. Her hands played along the soda can as she curled her legs underneath her and leaned back in her chair.

"Lieutenant Junior Grade."

"That means you finished college, then?"

"Yes."

"That must've been hard. All that school in between all those missions," she said.

"It wasn't that bad."

Her father's stories about his time in Baby-D, or Delta Force, were cool, definitely stirred Justin more toward the military than anything else. But Justin had grown up by the water, loved swimming, so the navy seemed like a much more natural choice.

He and Cash, his best friend on the team, had come up the ranks together. Cash had always been much more focused on school than Justin was as his mentor was an admiral, probably slated to be head of JAG one day. And Cash had insisted Justin keep pace with him on the classes.

Cash was a lieutenant who'd just made XO as Justin reached Lieutenant Junior Grade. In about two months' time, he'd earn his lieutenant stripes.

Turk kept telling him that he needed to come on over and work for the DEA—*better perks,* his friend would say. And Justin could just imagine what some of those perks were. But right now, Justin was pretty content in all aspects of his job.

Personal life—not nearly as content.

"You've got a lot of people worried about you, I'm sure. A lot of friends," she said, her voice wistful.

"So do you."

She shook her head. "No, not really. Besides Callie, what I've got for the most part are colleagues. Acquaintances."

"Your fiancé?"

"Oh. Forgot about him. I guess that break's pretty permanent now." She gave a soft laugh but he didn't join in.

"I know you were always more of a loner, more independent, but why did you shut yourself off?" he asked.

"It was easier that way. Helped with my focus. I knew what I wanted and I went after it. Not getting close with many people kept my path clear."

Coming from anyone else, that might've sounded ruthless. Coming from Ava, it was the opposite—her single-mindedness had always been her strongest trait, and it looked as if it was also potentially her biggest downfall.

She'd inherited that from her father.

"Tell me about your friends," she urged. "All SEALs?"

"A lot of them are. You spend so much time with your team, you tend to get pretty close."

"Leo's mentioned a few of them he's met. Hunt, I think—and Etienne…"

"Yeah, Hunt's great. He got married late last year—the wedding was on the beach—really cool. And Etienne's nicknamed Rev. Leo probably told you about the time we rode down to Daytona for Bike Week last year." Rev didn't have any interest in learning to ride a motorcycle, and Cash only wanted to go if he could surf. He and Rev rode down together in Rev's old pickup truck. Which, of course, broke down somewhere in Georgia.

"And Cash—he's your best friend next to Leo."

"He is. Manages to get into all sorts of trouble. Less now that he's practically engaged." He leaned back in his chair. "They're my family now. Sometimes I'll go to Rev's family's house in Louisiana for the holidays. Carly—Hunt's wife—had Thanksgiving this year. That was nice. Hunt's brother was really sick for a while, but it looks like he's going to be all right. That made it even more special, you know?"

"You really haven't spoken to your family at all?"

He'd been born and raised in Virginia—his family was from old money on both sides, powerfully connected in both business and social circles.

From the start, he hadn't been interested in his family's breeding and selling race and show horses. Their operation was set in the Shenandoah Valley and had been for several generations. His mother preferred to stay in the bigger cities where she'd been brought up and his father traveled back and forth. Meanwhile, Justin had concentrated on raising hell any way he could.

"There's nothing left to say to them." He shook his head as if that would clear out the strangely distant memories. It was as though someone else had lived his life for eighteen years, and he'd picked up at nineteen, after the year in limbo with Gina.

"Maybe they've changed."

He frowned. "They haven't. And that's all right. It's not about me."

"Suppose they've tried getting in touch with you? Leo told me that you're sort of not listed anymore. Anywhere, really, because of what you do," she persisted. "Maybe they'd be proud of you."

"I'm proud of me. That's all that counts."

"Were things that bad at home?" she asked.

He sighed. "Things were just…different at my house. Sterile. Cold. My brother and I never got along. We disagreed on everything from politics to his treatment of women. He took after my father in that way."

"In what way?"

"He slept with as many of them as he could. Lied to them

to get them into bed and threw them away as soon as he was done." He paused, then released a long breath. "I tried to warn them, some of them, but they didn't want to listen. James felt as entitled as my father did."

"Your father had affairs?"

"Lots of them." Justin had been ten the first time he'd caught his father with one of the maids. At that point, he'd known his family wasn't perfect, but he'd been away at school for most of his young life and kept the vision of a good strong family to get him past the loneliness.

He'd been home over Christmas break and came back to the house earlier than expected from the park around the corner. He hadn't felt well, had gone looking for his mother or father and heard the noises coming from the master bedroom.

He knew more about sex at that point than he should've, knew exactly what was going on in that room. He'd stood outside the door for a minute, recognizing the voices before going to his room, shutting the door and forcing himself to fall asleep.

God, he wanted to put it all to rest. Immediately, and forever. But the present had him more confused than ever.

He'd grown up with very few models of a good marriage. His old commander, Mac, and his wife were one. So were Rev's parents. They'd never officially married but they'd been together for almost twenty-eight years. Justin thought about the way they'd danced around the crowded kitchen, right in the middle of cooking dinner.

A totally different experience from the impersonal environment he'd grown up in, where the kitchen was off limits and his parents only showed affection in public, and even then, minimally so.

He wanted what Rev's parents had—his whole team did,

on some level, but the secrecy and dangerousness of their jobs precluded some of that.

Some, not all. Hunt had found happiness, so had Cash. It just took the right woman. And he still didn't have a gauge if Ava would nix the rest.

"You really love what you do," she said.

"Yes." He had to make that clear—crystal. It wasn't something he was ready to give up yet. Maybe never. But Ava would never ask him to choose. He knew she'd just make her own choice, and he didn't want to think about what that would be. "You can understand that, can't you?"

"All too well."

IT WAS THE CONVERSATION Ava had been hoping to avoid. Justin seemed to realize that, veered off it quickly, as if he, too didn't want to deal with the eight-hundred-pound gorilla in the middle of the room.

"From what your brother's told me, work's going well for you," he said instead.

"You mean, except for the fact that people are trying to kill me?"

He shrugged. "Someone's always trying to kill me when I'm at work, but that doesn't mean things aren't going well."

He was completely serious. So serious that she nearly spit her soda out at him. Instead, she choked it down and looked up to find him staring at her.

"What? You've never heard the expression 'If you're not pissing someone off, you're not doing something right'?"

"Then I guess I'm definitely doing something right."

"You are. I can't tell you how many times Leo won't stop bragging about you." He paused. "What do you think about more—the losses or the wins?"

"The losses, of course. Doesn't everybody?" she asked. The losses were what kept her up nights, pacing around, eating ice cream right out of the carton.

"No."

"Don't be a jerk."

"I'm telling the truth. I thought that's what you wanted," he said, throwing his hands up in the air. "If you don't stop worrying about what you didn't accomplish, you'll never get anything done."

"Oh good, boot-camp euphemisms."

"I can't do this every time we try to have a conversation," he said quietly. "I know you're still pissed at me for deserting you. You're pissed at your dad for dying, and probably the most pissed at Leo."

She hated it when he was right. She was more than upset about Justin's entry into the military, and when Leo had announced his intention to try for the DEA, it was one of the worst betrayals, next to Justin's.

"I thought you'd reconsider. You and Leo both. Instead, it's like you two are headed off on some mission to save the world."

"Not the entire world. Just a small section of it," he tried to joke, but her eyes blurred with tears and her throat tightened and she was suddenly so angry, more than she'd been when her mother left, more than when she'd gotten that phone call about her father.

They'd all left her. That's what people you loved did—they left for higher ground. So she ran out on them first.

She was still running. And helping other women to run, too. Except they were running to something, to safety. She was running with no end in sight.

"I know I don't have the kind of life you want, Ava. You've

always said that you didn't want to be a military wife, didn't want what your mom had. If we'd gotten together, then you might not have done everything you've done and want to do."

"And I might have. I should've been allowed to make that decision. But that's all a moot point, right?"

Still, when she'd been in his arms, none of the stuff they butted heads about—not his job or hers—mattered.

He wasn't saying anything, only sat calmly in his chair. Waiting.

"I've always depended on myself," she said finally. "I could turn to my dad and Leo when they were around. But it was easier—safer—to just depend on me. Especially after…"

"After I left," he finished. "You could always depend on me when I was there. But you kept testing and testing…" He paused, as if the lightbulb finally went on. "You did that on purpose, didn't you? You were just hoping I'd fail so you could prove yourself right."

"You left, Justin. You laid this bombshell on me, and then you left."

"What I did had nothing to do with you."

"It had everything to do with me."

"I was trying to do the right thing. To save my future. A friend would've understood."

She wanted to shake him, to tell him that she was so much more than a friend, but realized for the first time that Justin was fragile inside. That thought made her want to walk over and hug him, protect him from the world.

"I wished your dad was around during that time," he said. "He would've known what to do."

"My dad?"

"Your dad was awesome."

"When he was there," she said. She'd been so lonely, had

grown up so lonely that she hadn't recognized the aching feeling in her gut as unusual. In her family being alone and self-sufficient was considered normal. She'd carried that with her into adulthood.

"He loved you a lot. You knew that, right?"

"I knew that. I just wish he'd been happier."

"He'd have been really proud of you now. He always was. I mean, you knew what you wanted to do and you went out and did it."

"I guess so," she said. "I guess we're both a lot like him."

"Maybe we're not meant to do anything beyond work and a little play," he admitted.

She didn't disagree, but she didn't agree either. Instead, she changed the topic.

"So how do you turn the bad stuff off? Stay positive?" She balanced her chin in her hand, her elbow on the table.

"Sometimes I try not to think about it at all," he explained. "Other times, I think about something special, something really important to me. Something I'd hate to lose."

"And that's what gets you through?"

"That's what gets me through."

"What's the worst mission you've ever been on?"

"I can't tell you that," he said. "Some are more successful than others, but every time I step off the helo on my own steam means it was a success."

She nodded. Earlier, she'd taken the time to trace her finger over a few circular scars that ran along his back in an almost up-and-down pattern. Four of them. *Flesh wounds,* he'd joked, but his dark eyes had gotten darker and he'd pulled her in for another kiss so she wouldn't ask any more questions.

How does none of this show on you, she'd asked him

earlier, because she knew there were circles under her eyes, not as deep as they could've been, but a testament to the stress she was under.

If she continued to keep up the pace at her job, she'd burn out in no time.

Law school had been exhausting, nonstop hours of studying and performing, of proving herself to her peers and her teachers. Competing for the top-of-the-line internships.

In the end, she'd forgone the fame and fortune in order to serve what she considered to be the greater good. Which meant fighting for the people who had no one else to fight for them. She never felt the need for big money or for glory, but those internships had proven their purpose. She knew how those big corporations operated, and that gave her an edge in the D.A.'s office.

Again, her father's genes coming out in her.

Leo, well, she and Leo had broken the family tradition of military service. Her father's sister lived cross-country and she'd offered to take the two of them in after Ava's dad's death, but Leo refused. Since Ava was seventeen and Leo nineteen, there was nothing her aunt could do.

She'd managed to keep her smarts, her questioning skills up like a barrier around her. And she'd been completely successful at keeping almost everyone at arm's length.

God, how had she not realized before now what she'd been doing?

"You're too hard on yourself," he said.

"How do you do that? Read me so well, even after all this time…"

He shrugged. "It's not that hard if you know what to look for."

"I wish you'd kept looking…when your marriage failed."

"Me, too," he replied. "But what would've been the point?

You knew what you wanted. What you didn't want. By then, I was more than on my way to being it exactly."

A military man. Another man in her life on the edge of danger. But she did want him, so badly it hurt.

The worst part was, the only thing stopping her from having him was her. She had no idea how to get out of her own way.

13

JUSTIN HAD NO IDEA where to go from here and he was grateful when his phone rang. A little less grateful, however, when he saw who the caller was.

"Is it Leo?" Ava asked hopefully.

"No, it's not him." He watched her face fall. "It's only been a few hours…"

"Six hours."

"He'll call again," he reassured her, and then picked up the line that Rev was on the other end of. "What's going on?"

"I don't have much time to talk, Hollywood is so after your ass."

"Karen called him."

"Yeah, looking for you, claims you're not answering your phone and that you're interfering with a DEA investigation."

Shit. Shit. Shit.

"Cash's running interference for you, but Hollywood's not buying your dating-Ava story. He says that unless you come back here with a marriage license, he's not going to believe a thing you say."

"Hollywood not believing me is the least of my concerns."

"He said he's going to let the DEA charge you *and* he'll bring you up on charges himself. Disobeying a direct order. Which he's going to give you as soon as he stops lecturing

Cash about getting involved in Gray Ops missions to begin with."

Justin squeezed the bridge of his nose between his fingers, but that didn't stop the roar in his brain.

He was putting it all on the line. His career, his future, everything, including his heart, and all for Ava. Digging himself out of this one wasn't going to be easy. Turk had been right about that. Although Turk couldn't have known what he was asking Justin to do at the time.

Miracles did happen. So did nightmares. It looked like one was about to strike again.

Justin heard his CO's voice barking Rev's name, right before Rev whispered, "Gotta go, boo—stay clean, you hear?"

The phone rang almost immediately. He stared at the number, shook his head at Ava and decided to take this one. Might as well get all his spankings now, then go offline for a while.

"So you're finally answering."

"I've been out of range," he drawled.

"Cut the cute act, Justin. I've spoken with your CO." Karen's voice was harsh and no-nonsense.

"So I've heard. Thanks for that."

"There have been other threats," Karen told him. "You need to let us take Ava into—"

He closed the phone again, threw it on the table.

"Will you please tell me what's going on?" Ava asked.

There was no point in lying. "I'm in deep trouble."

"Because you didn't turn me in to the DEA."

"Right."

"I'll tell them that I refused to go. They can't make me go into custody."

He shrugged. "With a case like this, they might be able to.

At the very least, I was supposed to follow that order. And I refused. That was my choice as much as it was yours."

"Justin, I can't let you risk everything for me…I can't ask that."

"You didn't ask. I'm doing it." He thought about what Rev said. "My story about us dating though is sort of blown with my CO. He's covering for me, for now, but he said I have to bring him a marriage license or he'll bring me up on charges."

"Marriage? Like, you and me, married? Like that's ever going to happen."

Which wasn't exactly the reaction Justin ever wanted to hear from her, especially not with the memory of her arms wrapped around him still so fresh in his mind.

"I DIDN'T SAY it was going to happen," Justin said shortly. "You asked me to keep you informed, so that's what I'm doing."

"I didn't mean anything by that. I mean, it's just that I thought you were joking."

"Yeah, because I really joke about things like marriage. I guess us falling into bed earlier was a joke, too."

"I don't know…I don't know what any of this is. You've done so much for me." All the sacrifices, and all she could think about was herself, how much she could potentially lose.

"Yup, that's me. A real do-gooder. Ready to take on the world at a moment's notice," he snapped.

"I don't know what to say, Justin. I'm sorry, for all of it. You've been through a lot."

"Don't be. It's not your fault. The trouble with the DEA and my CO is firmly on my shoulders."

In an attempt to stop him from walking out of the room, she called out, "I know what it's like to be with someone, and not to be in love."

It worked. He didn't turn back, but his hands gripped either side of the doorjamb. He swayed back and forth, as if he could still bolt at any moment. And even though she knew he wouldn't go far, she didn't want him gone at all.

"Your fiancé?" he asked, saying the word as though it left a bad taste in his mouth.

"Yes. He was perfect for me. Everything I should want."

"So what was the problem?"

"He wasn't you," she whispered. This time, she was the one who fled, out of the kitchen and into the bedroom, slamming and locking the door behind her.

She took in deep, stuttering breaths, wiped her eyes angrily. She hadn't cried this much since her father had died.

They'd told her over the phone. No one from the DEA even came to the house. She'd never forgiven them for that. They'd had her father for the majority of her lifetime and they couldn't even come to the door.

And what was she doing now? She and Justin couldn't live here forever.

She'd tell him that he could take her in, that he could get on with his life. It was for his own good.

But she wouldn't put the burden on him. She'd make the call herself.

"I STILL DON'T KNOW your name."

Callie's words drifted over him like a cool breeze and for a long minute, Leo didn't know where he was and he didn't care, either. Only cared that her body was draped lightly across his, that his head and face felt better, his ribs moderately so, and that it appeared they were safe.

She stared up at him, her blue eyes daring him to answer. The only sign of nervousness was the slight tug of her full bottom lip. He leaned down and kissed her, more gently than he would have liked to, necessitated by his split lip.

She didn't fight him or push him away. Instead, she asked, "What was that for?"

"For being so damn brave."

"I'd say *anytime,* but I really don't want to get caught in a situation like that again. I know the only reason we got out of there is because you knew the place so well. Because you worked for them…but you're not like them."

"I'm not. And I don't work for them. Not really."

"You said you did."

"My name's Leo," he said, as if that explained everything, and she smiled and that seemed to satisfy her. "Who the hell are you, lady?"

"The lady who saved your ass," she whispered, right before she pressed a sweet kiss to his cheekbone.

"If I wasn't so hurt…"

"You'd take off my clothes right here and make love to me?"

"Am I that predictable?"

"You're a man."

"You say that like it's a bad thing."

"No, it's not, I guess. I'm sorry. I probably shouldn't have fallen asleep on you like that—it's too familiar."

"I think we're way past the point of familiarity. I'm naked in bed with you and by my account, we saved each other's asses a few times."

"Yeah, well, I've been threatened before. This was a pretty big one, though. If you hadn't been in that room…" She trailed off and drew her knees up to her chest.

"But I was. And I still am," he whispered as his fingers played with the buttons on her shirt. She didn't pull away or stop him, not even when he began to undo the buttons, one by one, until they were all open. A slow, tentative slide of his hand under the soft washed cotton and she was shrugging the shirt off her own shoulders, exposing full, beautiful breasts and a curvy figure he needed on him. Immediately.

"Slide down here, Callie…please."

She complied, ended up on her side next to him. Carefully, he eased himself up onto one elbow.

"You're going to hurt yourself," she said.

"It's worth it," he murmured, his mouth against hers. "So worth it."

"Lie back," she said.

"Only if you promise not to go anywhere."

She didn't answer him but he complied anyway, let her settle him against the pillows before she knelt next to him and began to unbutton her jeans. She leaned forward to kick them off and then she held herself over his body, barely touching him until he reached out and held her hips.

He needed more contact. "Come here, Callie. Closer."

She didn't protest again. Her body covered his, avoiding his hurt side as much as possible as their tongues met in a tangle of desire that was as hot as it was unlikely. Unexpected.

Where the hell did she come from? he thought to himself, briefly, before she sheathed him inside of her with a sudden, desperate need.

14

JUSTIN STOMPED AROUND the side porch in the dark for a few minutes, trying to rid himself of that, weight-of-the-world, feeling he'd come to despise. He'd given up on that whole self-pity thing a long time ago when he'd realized that it didn't do him any good and didn't change a freakin' thing. But this tendency to take over and make things better for everyone he thought he could help, wasn't going away as easily.

His back went up as soon as he'd started to breathe normally again, though, and he let his gaze slowly circle the perimeter of the property. Nothing.

Still, someone could be out there. His hand reached into the back of his jeans where he'd tucked his gun for safekeeping. He turned slowly and almost fell into that freakin' moat.

"I'm going to kill you," he said quietly. He lowered the weapon after a second and shook his head.

"I didn't know what was worse—sneaking up or barreling in," Rev explained. "I went for stealth."

"You went for giving me a heart attack." Justin automatically looked down the long road, even though he knew Rev was too good to be followed. The thing with Rev was, even though a certain brand of trouble seemed to follow him everywhere, it never seemed to put the team at risk. So Rev could arrive here safely, without issues, but Justin gave it half an hour before something stupid happened—like the porch collapsing.

When the floorboards creaked as Rev jumped the moat to get up onto the porch, Justin said a silent prayer.

"I parked a few miles back and came in through the woods." He reached out a hand to Justin and when Justin extended his own, Rev pulled him in for a hug. "It's good to see you."

"You shouldn't be here," Justin warned when he stepped away from the younger man. Rev was only twenty-four, the baby of their team, yet somehow he was more dangerous than any of the rest of them combined, when given the right opportunities. Although, the difficulty Justin was in now could lead to an entirely different type of danger. "It's a mess. You could get in trouble."

"That's why I'm here, instead of Cash."

Justin knew that Rev was thinking of leaving the team, moving on to other forms of Special Ops, while Cash had just been promoted. To involve Rev in this was bad enough, but to involve Cash would be much worse.

"God, this is so fucked, Rev. What the hell am I going to do?"

"Looks like you've already got some kind of plan cooked up."

"It's half-assed and you know it. You're only being nice not to say anything because you think I'm going to go off the deep end if you do."

Rev, being Rev, didn't deny anything.

"I'm in love with her," Justin blurted. "At first, I thought maybe it was because we'd never really given it a chance. Never did anything beyond an almost roll in the hay. Now I know that sleeping with her then would've made everything worse. Because when I was married to Gina I wouldn't have had the luxury of being able to tell myself that things wouldn't have worked out with Ava."

"And now?"

"Now I know a hell of a lot better."

"What are you planning?"

Justin's look must've said it all, because for a minute, Rev simply stared at him, then slowly nodded. "You're due back on base soon. I'm assuming you'll be there."

Justin didn't answer him. He and Rev just sat there, staring out into the woods. "Has any of this made the papers?"

"Not a hint," Rev told him. "It's like the whole story's been blacked out."

"That's a plus."

"It's not your fault if she's got to go into protection, Justin. You've done everything you could. And maybe the protection would only have to be temporary."

"You can't be sure of that. And besides, would you want to live like that—in protection? Never seeing anyone you cared about again?"

Rev didn't hesitate. "No, that's something I could never do. You couldn't either, I know that. But we're not everybody."

"Ava's made her own choice," Justin said. "She doesn't want to leave."

"Then you've got to see sense and be the strong one in this situation."

"You sound like Cash," Justin said.

"Yeah, well, he lectured me on the phone nearly the whole drive up." Rev smiled, and the two men laughed quietly.

Cash's voice had guided both of them home on more than a few occasions when the team had been separated, and he'd talked them through a new set of instructions, or found them a path to take to the nearest LZ when theirs fell under fire. Like all of the SEALs, Cash liked being in charge, was comfortable in that position, and for a minute,

Justin really wished he could just put him in charge of this whole situation.

Except he knew he hated Cash's solution already.

REV STAYED for an hour, just long enough for him to confirm that Justin hadn't made any kind of decision yet. His teammate had offered to stay behind, to take over, even, but Justin had refused.

When he went inside, he was glad to note that at least Ava had come out of the bedroom. She had her back to him and was staring at the television screen, unmoving and, judging by her stance, he knew something was wrong.

Over her shoulder, he watched the morning news vividly recap the brutal murder of a young A.D.A. in New York. An A.D.A. who'd taken over the O'Rourke case in Ava's absence.

Ava was barely breathing.

He crossed the distance to shut the TV off, but she still didn't move.

This mess had just gotten worse; was tightening like a noose around their necks.

He didn't like the look he saw in Ava's eyes. There was sadness, disbelief, shock—all normal and none of which bothered him. It was the defeat he saw behind all the other emotions, something he'd never, ever associated with Ava, and didn't want to.

He stood in front of her, gripped her arms hard enough to shake her out of her trancelike state. "Ava, that's not your fault."

"Leave me alone," she whispered.

"No."

"Leave me alone," she repeated.

"No."

Her gaze moved up to his face, but her eyes didn't meet

his. Instead, her hands came up, touched his cheeks, his lips, a finger along the outer ridge of his ear as if assuring herself that he was really there.

"Not your fault," he repeated.

"Shut up," she whispered. She impatiently brushed away a tear that threatened to fall and brought her lips to his. And as much as he wanted to resist, stop this like he knew he should, there was no way in hell he had that kind of willpower in him.

Her hands fisted in his hair and she was kissing him as if he was saving her life. They were hard, almost desperate kisses that left them nearly unable to breathe.

She needs this, he told himself. But he knew he was a liar, because he needed it more. Much more.

Finally, he tore his mouth away from hers.

Her breathing was ragged, but she began to yank his shirt open without bothering with the buttons, her hands running along his chest and still, still she wasn't meeting his eyes.

He didn't like that. If he was going to make love to her, she was damn well going to know it was him.

"Look at me," he said quietly. She ignored him, put a mouth to his nipple and sucked hard. She did the same to the other and he groaned. But he wasn't about to be deterred.

This time, she wasn't taking Justin the high-school boy, or Justin the hero, to bed.

Tonight, she was going to take Justin the man, and he would make sure that he erased the memory of everyone else but him from her mind.

"Look at me," he asked again and her head jerked up. Her eyes met his.

"Look at me," he whispered fiercely. "Look at *me,* dammit."

She stared at him, green eyes dark and steady. "I'm looking at you. I see you. I always have."

"Good." He drew her in close and let his mouth come down on hers to take away the fear and the pain, to make her forget everything, if only for a little while.

Yes, he would take control of the situation.

But she wasn't having any of it. Instead, she twined her fingers into his hair, yanking him to her and not so gently, either. He didn't mind, and he let her tug and push and slide her hot tongue inside his mouth in a way that left both of them breathless. She kissed him, deep and wet, demanding his full, undivided attention.

When he pulled back, they were both panting.

"Ava..."

"Get into bed, Justin. Now."

He bucked slightly at the command in her tone, thought about refusing for half a second.

The problem was, he could never actually refuse Ava anything, at least not for long. Especially not now, when she was giving herself to him and asking him to do the same. So he walked into the bedroom with Ava on his heels, stripping off his clothes as he went.

He turned to face her and she pushed him, hard, with the heels of her palms against his bare chest. Once, twice, until he sat on the bed and did as she wanted.

He let Ava use her tongue along his shoulder, his pecs then his nipples. His body jolted as if the hard pebble she rolled between her tongue and teeth was directly attached to his groin.

"Ava...Ava." He tightened one hand in her hair while the other palm rubbed the back of her neck.

It was his turn to close his eyes, to just let go and *oh yeah*, she was going to take him, ride him, do naughty things with him tonight and her hips. And he was going to come inside of her hot, wet sex over and over, because that's what they had to hold on to.

She guided him inside her in one slow grind that had him quickly steadying himself. As she continued to pump back and forth, she kept her eyes open and on his. Letting him know she was fully aware of what she was doing and who she was with.

The slow, delicious friction built to a fever pitch within minutes as Ava milked him. When her orgasm began, he held on as long as he could, until her eyes widened and her fingers clutched at his shoulders, and then he came, hard and fast.

They were bathed in each other's sweat. Ava untangled herself first, and scooted next to him. For a few seconds, she lay there, trying to catch her breath. But he turned to her just in time for her sobs to begin again.

"It'll be all right. I'm going to make sure of it," he told her.

"I know," she said softly. "I'm sorry I wasn't there when the bottom fell out for you."

"Right back at you, Ava. Right back at you."

"You're here now, though."

"Yes, I'm here."

"Has there…been anyone since Gina?"

"There have been a lot of someones," he admitted. "None of them special. I wasn't special to them, either. I made sure of that. It's hard enough having a relationship, but when women find out that you're not around much, that you're going to break dates and miss important stuff…"

"Seventeen years and my dad made it to three birthdays," she broke in.

"He was there when it counted."

"My birthday doesn't count?"

"Anyone can come through for a birthday or an anniversary.

I've never understood why people think those dates are so great. To me, it's the times in between that are the most important."

"He wasn't there then, either."

"He was there when you were in the hospital because your appendix burst. And there during that whole summer of your junior year, when we all went camping," he reminded her.

"When did you become so logical?"

"I was always logical. Did the motorcycle and the dancing on the bar fool you?"

She laughed quietly at the memory. "You were so wild. All kicked out of your fancy boarding school, the brooding bad boy. All the girls wanted you."

"All of them?" he asked softly.

"All of them. I'll bet all the girls *still* want you."

"I'm not interested in all the girls. I'm not interested in girls at all—just one woman. The same one I've been trying to shake from my mind for nine years." He spoke the words into the darkness, but hoped they reached her just the same.

"So why didn't you ever…try?" Her voice sounded far away, as if she was fighting sleep, and fatigue was about to win the battle.

He answered her anyway. "Fear. Pride. Lots of different reasons. So many times, I almost did. But like I told you before, I didn't know if it would matter."

"It always mattered. I love you, Justin. I always have."

She'd already fallen asleep by the time he whispered the same words back to her.

"SO, WHERE ARE WE?" Leo asked, even as he fought to catch his breath. He wasn't sure how long they'd lain there, wrapped together, recovering, but he was pretty sure the earth had moved. Twice.

Callie lifted her head off his chest and rolled partially off his body. "We're in Ohio. Small town, off the map. It's a safe house."

"Why would you know about safe houses?" he asked. "You're not in witness protection, are you?"

"No." She shook her head quickly, a little too quickly. Then she spoke quickly, as if saying what she had to say fast would somehow make him forget her admission. "I've just helped some women relocate. I work with a lot of domestic abuse cases and I don't normally talk about this stuff with anyone."

"I think we can probably trust each other at this point." He shifted on the bed and winced slightly. Yes, ribs healing was going to take much longer than twenty-four hours. "Were you…I mean…?"

"No. It was my dad. My mom was the one who caught all the abuse. At least she did until she took me and she ran. I was eight. I thought she was the bravest woman in the world."

"She's probably very proud of you and what you do." Most of Callie's work probably broke the law in some respect, which explained her guardedness. It also explained the eclectic collection of skills she'd acquired along the way. She was a woman who knew how to disappear and well.

"No, she'd be upset with me. Probably rightly so."

"Why's that?"

"Because I haven't given myself a chance at anything close to resembling love. She used to say to me, 'we've all given love a second chance, hon. Some of us five or six chances.'" Callie paused. "She died ten years ago."

"And now it's just you."

"Just me," she agreed quietly. "What about you?"

"I've got a sister," he said shortly.

"Are you guys close?"

He shut his eyes for a second, wishing he could give in to the driving need for sleep. "We're close. She's a pain in the ass, but we're close."

She laughed, a nice sound. "Family's important."

"Yes, family's important," he repeated, even as he grabbed his cell phone and rang the familiar number three times before hanging up. *All's right on this end, Justin.* "The woman who helped us in here…"

"She won't say anything to anyone. What would she say anyway? She doesn't know who you are any more than I do."

"It's better like that. For now."

She nodded, as if she didn't expect it to be better any other way. He promised himself he'd spend at least until dawn trying to make it otherwise.

15

JUSTIN SPENT the rest of the night watching the security cameras' feed and watching Ava sleep, and wishing he could wake her and make love to her all over again. Wishing she wasn't so upset.

He'd breathed her, let his body become a slave to hers all in the space of twenty-four hours. Not to mention the years he'd spent with her and apart from her. There was no way to get out of this cleanly, with any shred of sanity. She'd taken him to the brink of heaven again and again, and now he was supposed to give that up?

You could take her away from here yourself.

He'd had enough training, could easily blend in and start over with her in a new town, with a different identity. But that wouldn't be fair to either of them.

He was pissed at himself for getting upset with her, more pissed at himself for not thinking this whole plan through, for letting his emotions for Ava override everything.

In his work, there was no room for uncontrolled emotions. He'd learned that early on, in boot camp, had it reinforced through all of BUD/S training. He'd have to pull it back in order for this mission to succeed.

And that's exactly how he needed to start thinking about this—as if it was a mission. Which he would not fail.

In those final moments of indoc, affectionately known as Hell Week, when the majority of his BUD/S class had rung out, Justin knew that was not an option for him.

His group was down to four members and shit, they'd been dragging. Archer had a stress fracture in his left shin and Justin remembered his own feet being so battered and bloodied that he never thought he'd walk without pain.

It didn't matter in the end. None of it did.

He pushed past it, through 0300, 0400, 0500 and there it was, the most beautiful thing—sunrise.

Sunrise, and he was still standing.

He would not fail at this. He needed this.

None of the members of his current team were part of that ten-man crew who'd walked up the beach that morning, secured, but not yet SEALs. Still, Justin knew where each and every one of them was.

Two retired due to injury.

One retired from active duty but was the master chief of training out in Coronado.

One was KIA.

Five were stationed out in Coronado, still active duty with the teams.

And him. On the teams for the past six years, not counting the thirty or so months of training to get him his Trident pin. Long before that ceremony, he and Gina had fallen apart. One failure balanced by a success. Overall, he felt ahead of the game, and he was going to make sure it stayed that way.

On the porch, during his hourly surveillance, he'd almost called Cash but thought better of it. He and Ava were on their own until he said differently, and he honestly didn't want to say anything but *stay with me* to her.

He shoved the phone back in his pocket, ignoring all the

messages he saw piling up from Cash and Rev and, *shit,* from his CO and, having successfully avoided the moat Rev had dug on the south side this time, smelled coffee brewing inside the cabin.

He never expected to see an unmarked car, driven by Karen, pulling up in the early-morning light. He didn't bother to wait for her to park, didn't acknowledge her at all. He just slammed and locked the cabin door behind him and called for Ava.

AT THE SOUND of Justin's call Ava came running. She'd been dressing after a shower, wondering how to break the news to him. But she had a sinking feeling, judging by the look on his face, that she was too late. "What's wrong?"

"The DEA is here."

God, she hadn't expected them so soon. She'd called them from the bedroom yesterday, after she'd run away from him and before she'd seen news of the murder on TV. That only solidified her decision—she couldn't bring any more of this on anyone else, especially not Justin. "I called them," she said quietly. "They said they could track the signal here."

"Why would you do that?"

"Susie's coming back." Justin whirled around to stare at her. "She's coming back to officially give her evidence. That was always her plan. She knows how much she's risking, but she's doing it anyway."

"How is she getting to the city?"

"I told you, I don't know anything, Justin. I was going to show up for the grand jury hearing next week and pray."

"Is Susie Mercer really an abused woman?"

"She is. But that's not the only reason she came to me. The D.A.'s office was investigating her husband's activities. I didn't know he was tied in with the O'Rourkes until she told me."

"Ava—"

"Susie didn't really tell me anything yet. She didn't want me to become a target, the way she was. But she knows a lot of things—operations…she can topple everything."

"And you're going to be the one who cross-examines her."

"Yes."

"Is she the D.A.'s only witness?"

She shook her head. "No. We've got others, she's our best one. Our most compelling one. With her help, the D.A. is planning on taking on the O'Rourkes in a big way."

"So Susie is just going to waltz into an open courthouse? Have you thought any of this through?"

"Yes, I have. That's why I called the DEA. They said they can get me to the courthouse and watch out for Susie once she arrives. I'm sorry I couldn't tell you, Justin. I couldn't tell anyone."

"You're the only one who knows that this woman is coming back?" He ran his hands through his hair in obvious frustration. "Oh, wait, you probably can't tell me that, either. This is all alleged speculation on my part, right?"

"Don't tell me you haven't been there. I know your entire career's one big classified mission, just like Leo's. Just like my dad's. Don't you dare come down on me for doing my job."

"I have backing when I do my job. Team support. So does your brother. You've taken on all of this responsibility yourself and it's not working out all that well for you." He shook his head. "I get it. You don't trust me."

She was losing him as surely as she'd lost him all those years ago. But this time, she'd be forced to walk away. "I do trust you. I want you to go find Leo. Please."

"That's why you did this?"

"I know what I'm asking you to do could get you in more trouble."

"Could get *me* in more trouble?" He gave a short laugh. "What you're involved in is much more dangerous. And I'm not talking about your A.D.A. job."

"I can handle it."

"Like you're handling this?"

"This case is extreme."

"Why is all of this so important to you?" he asked.

"Martha Crafton's case changed me. Having to tell her that something she lived, breathed for a year before the trial came up…having to sell her out for the greater good… That pushed me too far over the edge."

"How did she handle it?"

"She didn't."

"Ava, all these women…helping them run, that's not going to get Martha back."

"I want it all to mean something."

"It does. As long as it means something to you, it means something. Don't you get that?" He paused. "You're not your mother."

"I know that. I've been avoiding being her for my entire life."

"By running from me."

"I wasn't running when I was seventeen."

His brown eyes stared her down. "You knew I was headed to the navy."

"I thought…I could change your mind," she sobbed. "I thought that, if you loved me, we could make things different together. I should have known better. People don't change."

"No, they don't. You haven't. You're still the same person I fell in love with. Then again, I never wanted to change anything about you."

His words hit her like a shot between the eyes. She'd been so busy concentrating on what he did, she'd nearly forgotten who he was. "You think we're the same people, but we're not. Things have happened to both of us."

But Justin was shaking his head, clearly not believing what she said. "Is that what you tell yourself when you think about calling me?"

"What do you tell yourself?" she retorted. "Because I'll tell you, I don't remember hearing anything at all from you. Not once."

"What good would it have done? We would've ended up here, in the same place, hopelessly attracted to one another, with you refusing to accept what I do for a living."

"Can you blame me?"

"No, I can't. But you can sure as hell blame me, can't you, Ava? Dammit." He stared at the floor for a second and then back at her, his eyes clear. "I'm sorry I wasn't there for you."

"Justin…you were—you *are* trustworthy and strong. My protector. The problem is, I didn't want to get used to your protection again. It was the same thing with my father and Leo…I've learned to protect myself now."

She didn't bother to point out that she certainly wasn't protecting herself now. Not physically, and certainly not her heart.

He didn't call her on that, though.

"So, this guy you were engaged to—you were the protector in the relationship? The one who carried the big guns—the balls?" he asked.

"That's not funny."

"I'm not trying to be funny. In a relationship, you're supposed to protect each other. It's not a one-sided deal. At least not all the time."

"What do you know about relationships?" she asked,

wishing she could take the words back as soon as they came out of her mouth.

But it was too late. His expression hardened the way it had when he'd talked about his marriage. "No, you're right, Ava. I don't know anything about relationships at all."

"Justin, I didn't mean…"

But his hand was up and he was walking away. She knew better than to push it right now and yet, she did it anyway, followed him, grabbed his arm and yanked him around to face her.

"You know what I remember, Justin? I remember being there for every single one of my father's deployment days, before he made Delta Force. Those were hard enough. Waiting for him to get on the bus. Watching my mother try not to break down in the car. But after—after, when he couldn't tell us, when every day with him left me wondering if he was going to be there when I got home from school, or when I got up in the morning…those times were even worse. And that's what it would be like, wouldn't it?" Her voice shook. Fear and anger and sadness combined to create a potent mixture of emotion that she could no longer hold back.

"Some couples say it makes them closer. That they don't waste time on all the day-to-day bullshit. That they appreciate each other more than people who don't deploy."

"Oh, right. I know all about that. All about the fact that I'm supposed to pretend everything's great and keep it all inside so I don't send you away upset. I'm supposed to take one for the team."

"You're not supposed to take anything, Ava. You're not part of a team, my team. You've made that clear. I get it. I can't convince you. I love you, you know that. But in this case, it's not enough for you. And as much as I want to, I can't change it."

"No, I guess you can't." Slowly she turned away from him and found herself walking out the door toward the woman she supposed was the DEA agent who knew Leo.

"I'm Ava," she said, and extended a hand toward the tall blonde who waited by the nondescript town car.

"I'm Karen and you're going to be fine," she told her, then touched her shoulder reassuringly.

Ava nodded, suddenly stoic. "I know I will."

Justin had followed her out; she could feel his presence behind her. But she didn't turn back around. Instead, she pointed toward the car and Karen nodded.

She got in, slammed the door and stared straight ahead before she lost what little was left of her resolve.

SOMEWHERE DEEP in his heart, Justin had known from the beginning of this mission-gone-wrong that in order to save Ava, he'd have to give her up.

He hadn't known it was going to rip out his heart.

He walked away from them and ran his hands through his hair.

"Take care of her, Karen," he said over his shoulder, hating the way his voice broke.

"Nothing but the best, Justin," she replied. He waited until the car was all the way down the driveway before sitting heavily on the edge of the porch.

He wasn't sure how long he'd sat there staring into space. It could've been a minute or an hour, but the numb feeling in his body wasn't getting any better and his heart just freakin' ached.

The thought of driving himself out of here, back to base and then to deal with the fallout, seemed entirely too much, and he wondered what would happen if he just stayed here.

A rustle from the woods made him look up to see Rev crashing through the bushes, carrying a sleeping bag and seeming no more the worse for wear from sleeping outdoors all night.

"You stayed," Justin concluded.

"I stayed," Rev agreed. "You did the right thing by letting her go."

"Then why do I feel like shit?" Justin asked.

"Doing the right thing always hurts. That's how you know it's right." Justin's thoughts went immediately to Turk and Rev lit a cigarette. "I'm going to grab a shower, and then I'll take you to base so you can check in."

Justin didn't bother to argue. He merely nodded then took a drag from Rev's cigarette and wondered if things would ever feel right again. He told him, "I'm not going to base yet." Rev stopped walking toward the door. "She doesn't want me. She just wants me to find Turk."

Rev sat back down next to him. "Any idea where he is?"

Justin stared at the phone. "Yes, if there's a way for you to trace this number."

"There's always a way, Justin. Always a way."

16

LEO PULLED his clean T-shirt and jeans on. He was stiff and sore as hell, but he was a million percent better, and the long, warm shower—with Callie—had helped.

He took a quick inventory of his belongings. Phone battery—dead. Cash/Credit cards—zero. Bullets—two. Knife—one.

A woman next to him he wanted to get to know a lot better. Check.

Not terrible odds.

"I have to figure some things out. For my work," he said as he watched her towel the moisture out of her long hair. She'd perched on the edge of the bed, dressed in a black sweater and jeans. Her sneakers were already on, but whether she thought she was going with him or not was something he wondered while he waited for the inevitable questions. He even had some himself. But she kept silent. "I know why you were kidnapped, Callie. You're involved in Susie Mercer's disappearance." It was the first time they'd discussed any of this since briefly mentioning it when they were being held at the O'Rourke compound.

"I don't know where she is," Callie started. "Susie came to me about a month ago. She wanted to get out of her marriage. And she had a lot of information about her husband's family she wanted to share with the D.A.'s office.

I went to an A.D.A. that I'd worked with before—I knew she'd be sympathetic to Susie's domestic issues—and that she could advise us on the information Susie had."

"And the A.D.A. did."

"There's a grand jury hearing next week. Neither the A.D.A. nor I know where Susie went, but we promised we'd be there to meet her when she comes to testify." Callie wasn't lying about any of it. That he was sure of.

"I'll take you back. Make sure that you're protected…"

But she was shaking her head long before he'd finished. "You don't understand, Leo. I'm not sure that I'm going back."

"What are you talking about?"

"With everything that's happened, I might not be effective in what I do. I've been tagged. It's not so much that I'm worried about the O'Rourkes. That will die down—no pun intended—once this whole Susie Mercer thing is taken care of. But the organization I work for could be exposed. And I can't take that chance. They've all worked so hard."

"I'm not leaving you here."

"You don't have a choice. Take the car—I won't need it."

"Hey," he said, but she'd already thrown the towel down and had started stuffing things into a bag. And she was ignoring him.

He touched her shoulder, but she jerked away from him. "Please look at me, Callie."

"Don't make this harder than it has to be."

"I'll come back for you. Can't you just wait here? Let me do what I need to do and then we'll figure something out?"

"You don't even know me. Why would you want to do that?"

"I don't know. There's something…something here. Don't tell me you don't feel it."

She bit her bottom lip again, the now-familiar gesture tugging at him more than it should. "I don't feel it."

"I thought you'd be a better liar."

"I've never had to lie about that before."

Now, *that* he believed. Especially when she pulled away from him again and continued to tuck things into the black duffel bag. He asked, "Is there a phone I can use without attracting any attention?"

"There's a prepaid cell on the kitchen table. Feel free." She turned to give him a small, tight smile.

He'd figure this out once he'd made his call. He dialed the familiar number and Justin picked up on the fourth ring. "Where the hell are you?" his friend demanded.

"Where are you? Where's Ava?"

"I'm in Virginia. Ava's all right." Justin paused. "She's with Karen."

"The DEA has her?"

"They wanted to put her under protection. She called them. Karen came and got her this morning."

"Get her back, Justin. I don't care what you do or how you do it—just get her back."

"How the hell am I supposed to do that, Turk? Karen's pissed at me and I'm in deep shit with my CO. In another few hours, I'm UA. And all Ava wants is for me to find you."

"Yeah, well, I'm not lost."

There was a long pause on the other end of the phone, and then he heard something in his best friend's voice he'd heard before, a long time ago. So long ago he almost couldn't place it. "Fuck you, Leo. Just fuck you, all right? And as long as you're not lost anymore, clean up your own mess this time."

"Justin—wait." Leo listened, didn't hear the click, but still there was dead silence between them, and his friend's anger was palpable. "I'm sorry, man. What happened? Did Ava give you a lot of hassle?"

"Nothing I couldn't handle."

Leo closed his eyes for a second and thought about the pain he heard in Justin's voice. "You still love my sister."

"Why do you need me to get her away from the DEA?"

"Answer me, Justin."

"Why? What does it matter now? Just tell me."

"I'm not letting you go UA. You're right. I shouldn't ask that of you. I'm not going to be the one who presses your back to the wall."

"It's for a damn good reason, Turk. I'm just…it's been a long couple of days."

"I think someone in the DEA blew my cover and leaked it, and Ava's identity, to the O'Rourkes."

"It can't be Karen."

"No, but it might be someone she's called onto the case. I've been under for three months so I don't know a lot of what's happening back in the office." He paced the floor as he gave Justin the location of the three safe hotels the DEA typically used as a first line of defense for people's limited-time protection. He'd do everything to get there himself, but Justin and Rev were much closer—they could be at the hotels within an hour.

And just like that, he and Justin were all right again.

Now Leo clicked the phone shut and shoved it into his pocket. "Callie, look, I don't think it's right for you to stay here. I don't have a choice. I'm going to take you back with me."

Dead silence greeted him, and he could tell by the feel of the house that he was the only one left inside of it.

17

THE HOTEL ROOM was a tight box. It came complete with a steel reinforced door, which the DEA installed in each of its special hotel rooms, and an armed guard who sat in the next suite. A spring-trap locked Ava from the inside, as if it would never let her out. She'd never been claustrophobic in her life, but here, she could definitely develop the phobia. And a few others, like extreme paranoia.

At least it distracted her, momentarily, from the pain in her heart.

All she had with her were a couple of pairs of underwear, three T-shirts, jeans and pajamas. One pair of cheap sneakers and the barest of bathroom essentials. Karen had promised her more soon, but all her time had been devoted to keeping Leo's end of the mission going, and Ava was happy to have her comforts come second in relation to that.

No one was going to give her comfort where she needed it most of all, though, and she'd been up half the night to avoid dreaming about Justin. She'd fallen asleep briefly that afternoon, right after she'd gotten settled in, and the dream was so real that she'd been sure he was right beside her in bed, his arms around her.

She'd begun a slow pace around the room as she thought about Justin. Strolling around the bed and the small desk in a figure eight, she wished she could at least open the shades to let the outside world in, no matter that it was night.

She was disoriented. And scared. And when the knock on the door came, she walked toward it briskly, more than grateful for the five minutes of companionship Karen would bring her. That, and hopefully news of Leo.

But it wasn't Karen at the door at all. "Ms. Turkowski, I'm Agent Coleman Harris. I've been working on the O'Rourke case with Leo and Karen."

He held up his badge so she could read it through the peephole. And then she opened the door.

Coleman Harris was tall, with a shaved head, steel-blue eyes and a commanding presence. She wasn't sure she felt safe anymore, although these days, safety was a relative term. But he held bags of food, and she was starved physically and for company.

"Come on in." She stepped aside to let him pass and he walked in but waited for her to lock up behind him. Then he set the bags down on the table in the corner of the room.

"You must be hungry," he said. "Sit and relax. We're not changing hotel rooms for another couple of hours."

"Oh, right." She'd forgotten that Karen had mentioned staying in the same place too long wasn't a good idea, at least not until the grand jury proceedings next week. "Thanks for the food." She sat at the small table and unwrapped a sandwich, but suddenly she didn't feel much like eating.

"You've had some tough times the past few days, but you really need to keep up your strength," he said.

"Have you heard anything about Leo?" she asked.

He shook his head. "He hasn't checked in. However, our reports indicate he's gone from the O'Rourke residence."

"Okay, well, that's something." She thought it was slightly

odd that Justin knew more about Leo's location than the DEA did at this point, but maybe Karen was keeping a tight leash on everyone.

"Karen wants me to take some notes on what you know about Susie Mercer," he continued.

"Oh. She didn't mention anything about that." So far, Karen had asked only the basics, but it made sense that they'd want to know more as they got closer to the grand jury trial.

"I know you can't tell us much, but if you could just give me a brief overview of how it all started…the DEA's involved in the case now. It's going to get complicated. We need to work together."

"Well, she first approached me in my office." It had been late—after six—although Ava hadn't been surprised to see the pretty woman at her door. There were a lot of people who wanted to bring their cases forward but were scared. Many of them waited outside the office all day trying to get their nerve up, only doing so when the place was nearly deserted.

But Susie hadn't been alone. "Susie came with Callie Stanton, she's a social worker who first spoke with Susie."

"She's also missing."

"Yes."

"Okay, keep going." Coleman made a few notes she couldn't see on his pad and she shifted, uncomfortable being the one not asking the questions.

Susie had been nervous, yet she'd told the first part of her story to Ava with such conviction that Ava had no doubt it was the truth. Instead of continuing the meeting in Ava's office, they later met at Callie's apartment, and Susie told them the story of her abuse and the way her husband tied in with the O'Rourkes.

"In the beginning, it was glamorous," Susie had admitted. "I was really young and poor and Robert showed me a life I never dreamed of. And for the early years, it was all right. I managed to pretend that what he did wasn't illegal, wasn't horrible."

"She gave us a lot of details about the organization. Things an outsider couldn't possibly know. She was around for the day-to-day dealings. She had access to computer files."

Coleman shook his head. "The grand jury could see her as a vindictive woman out for revenge."

"There's no way that would happen. Trust me," Ava said.

"Any word from Susie Mercer?"

"No. But she's supposed to show for the grand jury hearing next week."

"If she testifies, she can break this entire case wide open."

"She can and she will," Ava said. "Between what she knows about her husband's dealings, plus the bigger picture...the O'Rourkes don't have a chance."

"Susie took a huge risk running the way she did."

"She didn't have a choice. She didn't trust anyone."

"Neither did you. You could've gotten Leo killed."

"You don't need to tell me that. Don't you think I know that?" She shoved away from the table.

"I'm sorry, Ava. I didn't mean..."

"Once I meet Susie, once she testifies, everything she says will only help Leo's investigation."

"Do you know what she's going to say?"

"Some of it."

He leaned forward, elbows on the table, hands clasped together. "Ava, I know it's privileged. But we've worked so hard on this case. Leo's lived and breathed it for so long. If she's got information that can bring the O'Rourke family down..."

"She does," she told him. "Even though her husband flew under the radar, he was still involved in all their corruption and worse. By using his company, they were able to work on a much larger scale."

"So they were laundering money through Mercer's company."

"Seems so. Susie said she had specifics—paper trails and more."

"She couldn't have gone too far."

"Leo always said the best hiding places could be found close to home," she said.

He nodded, looked toward the door and frowned. "You've got valuable information."

"It's privileged. And secondhand."

"But if Susie doesn't show?"

She swallowed hard. "There are other witnesses I could call. Again, they don't know nearly as much as Susie and it's secondhand information, too."

Coleman Harris sighed. "We've put in a long time on this case. I'd hate to see it go up in smoke."

"It won't," she assured him, wondering why she was plagued by such an overwhelming feeling of unease.

"You're a very brave woman. Leo always said that about you."

"It's my job."

"What you did was above and beyond."

"Maybe. But Susie's part is more dangerous than mine."

"You could easily be used to draw Susie in," Coleman said, even as he stood. She did the same, automatically. "She's not going to show herself until she sees you."

"Or Callie Stanton," Ava admitted. "She was taken by the O'Rourkes around the same time that Leo was made."

"It's time to move you now," Coleman said.

"But I thought—"

"We're doing things a little off schedule to keep everyone on their toes."

"I'll just grab my things then," she said, unable to shake the dread bearing down on her. And while Coleman made a quiet phone call, she wished she had her own weapon.

"Agent Harris, I'd like to speak with Agent Karen Hamilton before I go."

He stared at her for a second, and she waited for him to tell her no, that wasn't possible. Instead, he gave her a small smile. "Let me grab her for you."

He left the room and she continued packing the few belongings she had and then she waited, sitting on the edge of the bed.

After fifteen minutes, she picked up the phone and did something she'd been told not to do. She dialed Justin's cellphone number, and let it ring until the knock at the door startled her.

She hung up quickly and walked over to peer through the peephole. She saw Karen's ID and opened the locks. Her brain told her, *wrong,* a second too late, and Agent Harris and another man easily pushed their way inside.

"What's going on here?" she demanded, although, in the face of the guns they held on her, she knew that wasn't going to get the answers she wanted.

Coleman Harris spoke as he grabbed her bag off the bed. "It's time to move hotels, Ava. And Mr. O'Rourke and Mr. Mercer will both be very pleased to see you. Unfortunately, your brother and your friend won't be able to make the party. Or any other parties. You, however, have proven to be even more valuable than we originally thought."

18

THERE WAS ABSOLUTELY no place for Ava to run to. Instead, she took two steps back to put some distance between herself and the two men, even as one of them barked for her to stay put.

She didn't obey and took another two steps back. *You're too valuable for them to kill you.*

At least, not yet. Until Susie took the stand, Ava was a hot commodity. "What the hell do you want from me?" she asked in an attempt to stall.

"You know exactly what we want." Coleman Harris closed the distance between them. Too close. She couldn't let him touch her.

"You'll never get me out of here."

"It's my job to escort you to the next hotel by whatever means necessary. So you can see just how simple this is going to be."

She saw a syringe in his hand and took another step back. She hit the wall and could go no farther.

"Just grab her and let's get out of here," the second man growled. "This job is screwed up enough as it is."

The click of a gun made Ava start, made the two men in front of her freeze.

She hadn't heard the door open, had never, ever expected

to see Justin behind them. A cold hard look of determination enveloped his face.

"Drop them," was all he said, and the men didn't have a choice. Mainly because Justin had a gun in each hand.

He was not fooling around, and she forced herself to stay upright. Now was not the time for a distraction.

Each man took the magazine clip from his gun and tossed it first, then dropped the weapon.

"Grab them, Ava," Justin instructed. She did so, gathering up the pieces and backing away from the men as the commotion in the hall increased.

Within minutes, Karen was in the room, her own gun drawn. "Are you all right, Ava?" she asked.

"Yes, I'm fine."

Karen was only half listening, was too busy staring at one of the men. "Agent Harris?" she asked, but there was really no question.

"Agent Harris?" Justin repeated as Karen helped him to cuff the men. Karen nodded and motioned to the men at the door.

"Take these two away. House them separately. I'll be the one interrogating each of them," she said. Once the door closed behind them, she turned to Ava. "Are you sure you're all right?"

"Yes. But I don't understand… What does this mean?"

"It means we've caught the leak in our department," she said. "The one who blew Leo's cover."

"So it wasn't me. Wasn't my fault, then?" she asked.

"No, it wasn't."

"Callie…oh my God, have you heard anything about her or about Leo?"

"Leo's all right. So is Callie," Justin spoke before Karen could, but even so, Ava noted the daggers aimed straight at him coming from Karen's eyes.

"Good, that's good," she murmured, hadn't realized she'd been slowly sinking to the floor until Justin's arms wrapped around her. She pressed her face to his chest and held on for dear life and just inhaled and exhaled, like he told her to.

One minute, she was merely breathing and the next, she was kissing him and wouldn't let go, not even when she heard Karen calling out her name first, and then Justin's. And then Ava heard the door shut again and she lost herself in the taste of him. Her hands ruffled through his hair, ran down his back and arms, as though she was checking to make sure that he was really here.

"Justin," she said against his mouth. "Please hurry…"

She wasn't sure what she was begging for, exactly, beyond his body on hers, but he was anxiously pushing himself away from her even as she pressed herself more closely to him.

She didn't care that a force of DEA agents were right outside the door. She only cared that she had Justin here and now and she was in his arms.

That was all that mattered, what it all boiled down to.

Justin didn't seem to care that people were outside the door, either, not the way he was tugging at her jeans and pulling off her top, whispering, "Beautiful, always so beautiful, Ava."

No, nothing else mattered but the heart-stopping way he took her—as if she was already claimed as his and there was no going back. His hands traveled along her back, bringing her against his body even as she was helping to take off the rest of his clothes.

He kicked his jeans impatiently off his feet and to the side and then there was no further barrier between them. His tongue teased hers and then his kisses deepened, until she knew she'd lose her balance if she let go of him. Her fingers dug into his shoulders and he lifted her so she was legs off the ground and wrapped around his waist.

One swift move and they were on the bed, limbs entwined, Justin entering her, moaning that he couldn't wait.

They'd been separated for just under twenty-four hours, but her body took him as if he'd been gone for much longer. Her legs remained locked around his waist, forced him more deeply inside her. It was obvious that neither of them would last long based on the near-frantic coupling, and she wasn't surprised when her own orgasm gripped her quickly. Justin's wasn't far behind, and the look on his face was one of complete peace and pleasure. His eyes were closed and a smile of contentment played on his lips.

She lay there under his weight, momentarily spent but nowhere near satiated, one hand stroking the back of his neck as his face pushed against her shoulder, his body still buried in hers.

There was movement outside the door. Her arms tightened instinctively around Justin's back, even as he lifted his head, to call out, "Don't come in here," in a tone so full of authority that all talk outside the door stopped.

"Justin, we need to—"

"I said, not right now, Karen."

There was no further argument. And so he turned his attention back to her, smiled in a way he hadn't done when she'd left him at the cabin.

He'd forgiven her. There was no way he could look at her like that, the way he used to when they were teenagers—the way he had after he'd made love to her for the first time the other night—and not love her.

But before she could ask him anything, a familiar phone

began to ring and the tension in the room immediately grew between them.

Justin rolled away from her, searching the floor for his discarded jeans. He glanced at the phone and then back at her before he flipped it open.

"Brandt," he said and turned his back to her. She saw the change in his posture. "Yes. I understand, sir."

He turned back to her. "I'm sorry."

"For what? Because you have to go?"

"For everything. For you and me, the fact that nothing happened sooner than it did."

"But it's happened now."

He shook his head. "I've got to go. Another hour and I'm UA."

"Is that what the call was about?"

He stared at her for a long moment, as though trying to memorize the scene. "No, that's not what they called to tell me."

He wasn't just being called in, he was being called in for duty. Moving out to parts unknown. All of them dangerous. None of them anything she could know about.

"I'm sorry," he repeated as he pulled on the rest of his clothes.

She put hers on as well, even as she tried to pull him toward her again, to regain that moment they'd just lost in the space of a few seconds.

"We can't do this. Not again." He held her at arm's length until she jerked out of his grasp.

"You came back here to get me. You can't tell me that what just happened didn't mean anything."

"Of course it meant something…it meant everything. But I'm trying to save both of us from unnecessary heartache," he said. "And as hard as I try, I can't make it work for you."

"You've saved my life once already. You can do anything."

"But I can't, Ava. I'm just a man."

"You're not *just* anything."

"Yeah, I am. That's all I've ever wanted to be—just some woman's man." He smiled, but it was small and tight and his handsome features were pulled taut, showing his pain.

"I love you," she told him. Because she did, and because that had to count for something. For everything.

"You don't love me. You love the old me. And I'm not him anymore."

It was happening again. The same words. The same two people. She forced herself to stay glued to the spot in front of him and not walk away. Tears welled in her eyes because she didn't want to be apart from Justin anymore. She'd tried it for years and it obviously never worked.

"Why are you saying this? You know you're in love with me. I heard you say it to me, even though you thought I was already asleep."

He didn't deny it. "I guess sometimes that's not enough," he said quietly.

"So that's it? This is just over? You're going to walk out of my life—again? Just like you did nine years ago?"

"Twenty-four hours ago, you walked out of mine. You made your decision. You tried it all on for size and decided that it couldn't possibly work for you. And I'm all for trying to accomplish the impossible, but there are only so many times I can bang my head against a brick wall before I learn. And I've learned, Ava. Dammit, I've finally learned."

His voice was so raw sounding, his posture unrelenting. "Justin…"

"I've got to be back at the base. In an hour, I'm UA," he repeated. "I'll make sure Karen takes you to the next hotel. Until it's time to testify, I'm guessing you're still in this. Still needing protection. I just can't be the one to do it anymore."

He hesitated for a second, then pulled her against him again, kissing her, hard and desperate, before walking out the door. And she wondered why, for the first time in her life, she felt like she was admitting defeat.

19

"YOU'RE GOING to catch your death of cold out here, walking in this weather. You should have let me pick you up closer to the house." Serena fussed over Callie, who sat wrapped in a blanket. Serena had been fussing since she'd picked Callie up hours earlier at the edge of town in the pouring rain.

"It's May. No one catches their death of cold in May." Callie punctuated that sentence with three sneezes and avoided glancing at the mother figure who would surely be glaring at her with the I-told-you-so look.

"Drink this tea. All down, no arguments." Serena sat opposite her on the couch. "Where did your green-eyed man go?"

Callie almost told her that his name was Leo, but decided against it at the last minute. She liked being the only one to have that piece of information. "Back where he came from."

Back where she wasn't going. She'd called Ava a few times but hadn't left any messages. It was probably better that way—a clean break. Callie could move on to the next town or city and pick up where she'd left off. Just another harried social worker doing her job.

"And you're not going to see him again? Just going to sit there and moon over him?"

"It's ridiculous, Serena. I've known him…scratch that, I knew him for all of twenty-four hours."

"I knew my ex for ten years before anything happened and look how that turned out," Serena reminded her. "Time means nothing. It's how you feel that counts."

"It's just…not the right moment for this."

"Love is supposed to be inconvenient, honey."

"I'm not talking about love, Serena," Callie protested.

"Sure you are. You just don't know it yet. So drink your tea and rest."

"I don't even know anything about him," she mumbled obstinately at Serena's retreating back. But she did know the way his body felt against hers, the way he held his breath for a minute when he came. The way he hadn't looked at her with anything but admiration on his face when she'd told him what she'd been doing with her life.

"You're not going to be able to keep this up forever," Serena had told her earlier.

"What do I do then?" she'd asked.

"You become part of the chain. A simpler part. So you can have a life. You deserve that."

Last night she could have sworn Leo was outside the house, leaning against the fence. She hadn't told that to Serena.

Sometimes, if you want something badly enough, you can almost make yourself believe it was true.

And that was exactly what had happened between her and Leo.

What he'd awakened inside of her in such a brief period of time was something she wouldn't be able to fit into the neat little world she'd created for herself. The one where love existed only for other people, not her, and the one where she existed to help women put their lives back together again.

Maybe it's time you put your own life together.

She closed her eyes and let her mind drift to the memory of being back in the safe house, lying next to Leo...

The first time she came was almost painful—exquisitely so, because she couldn't remember the last time her body had contracted like that. She'd collapsed, forehead against Leo's chest, his arms around her, but he wasn't done. In fact, she hadn't stopped shuddering before he was thrusting his hips up to drive himself into her again, was murmuring her name as if saying a prayer only he could understand.

And suddenly, nothing else mattered but the two of them together on that double bed that held the dreams of so many people who'd been there before them.

It was a lot like the time she'd gone on the big roller coaster when she was too young to do so. She was thrilled and exhilarated, heart in her throat and white-knuckling it all the way.

Now she sneezed again and again, and was actually grateful that she could blame her watery eyes on a cold, rather than a newly broken heart.

ARMED WITH the information from Justin, Leo called Karen and told her not to move Ava until he'd arrived.

A few hours later, he knocked on the door and waited for his sister to identify him through the peephole.

Within seconds, the door was open and she was hugging him and yelling at him all at the same time. When he pulled back, he noted she'd been crying, but the tears weren't fresh ones shed for him.

He had a pretty good idea who they were for, though. But first things first. "Are you all right? You've been through hell."

"I've been through hell? Look at you—your face—who did

this to you?" she asked, even as she yanked him over to the bed and sat down next to him.

"Part of the job," he said. "I'm sorry, Ava. Sorry about everything."

"You didn't know," she said softly. "I'm just so glad you're okay. I was really worried, but Justin—he always knew you'd be all right."

"Yeah, well, best friends are like that." He saw the flash of pain in her eyes. "Your friend Callie—she's all right, too."

"You were with her?"

"She was a big help in getting me out of trouble," he admitted.

She smiled. "Sounds like her. Where is she now?"

"She's, um, missing. Sort of. Took off on her own. But I'll find her."

"Why? I mean, I want you to, but is she still in danger?"

"Only from herself. Kind of like you."

Ava punched him in the arm lightly. And then she paused and stared at him, eyes narrowed slightly. Lawyer mode, like she'd been doing since they were little. "You like her."

"She's all right." He stretched out his legs on the bed and realized how much he missed sleeping.

"No, I mean, you *really* like her. Does she know?"

He thought about the way she'd stared at him right before she disappeared. "Yes, she knows."

They sat in comfortable silence for a few minutes before Ava spoke again. "She sometimes mentioned moving to Ohio. Some small town. She said it was peaceful. Nothing like New York. Do you think that's maybe where she is?"

"Could be." He put his head against the pillows and wondered if she'd only gone as far as the next house or the edge of town. Yeah, as if it would be that damn easy to find Callie. "She's a tough one, isn't she?"

"Yes, she's tough. You might almost be tough enough to handle her."

That made him smile, mainly because it was true. "Think she'll come back to New York with me?"

"I think you're the first and only guy who's got a shot, from what you told me."

"What about you and your shot with Justin?"

She chewed her bottom lip thoughtfully. "I had my chance. I let it go."

"How come?"

She paused. "It was the right thing to do."

"Right for whom?"

"Both of us."

"So you're happy with the decision, then?"

"I tried to change my mind… I did change my mind. But by that point, it was too late. Justin said he's done. That he doesn't want this to linger on and on without resolution. That obviously the barrier between us was too high to climb."

"That doesn't sound like the Justin I know. Not at all. And he also knows how you are once you've made up your mind about something."

"I *have* made my mind up."

"So why are you sitting here with me instead of being with him? Because he told you you'd never be ready?"

"Yes."

"But you just told me he's wrong about that."

"I know what you're trying to do, Leo."

"Is it working?"

"Yes," she said, and they both laughed. "Go get Callie. Stop her from running all the time. She's been in so many places and helped so many women. She deserves to be happy."

"We all deserve that."

JUSTIN MADE IT to base and his CO's office with only minutes to spare. His team wasn't moving out that day, but sometime within the next forty-eight hours.

Hollywood barely glanced up from the pile of papers on his desk. "This is for you."

A thick file, with classified intel for Justin to memorize in a hurry. He flipped through the folder as he stood in front of Hollywood, glancing through page after page of maps and co-ordinates, which he'd need to plan.

"When?" he asked.

"Immediate. Do that before you hit training. And get cleared by medical."

Yes, Justin could do that. All of that was ten times easier than thinking about leaving Ava behind.

WHERE DO I go from here?

Ava had been thinking these words for hours, since Justin had left, but hadn't realized she'd actually spoken them out loud until Karen had answered her. They were in Karen's car, driving to the new hotel Ava would be housed in, and, as Karen promised, guarded by her personally.

And now, Ava had *that* conversation repeating inside her head. Karen told Ava in one breath that they didn't know where Leo was at the moment, but they assumed he was safe, and in the next, that the DEA wanted to hire her.

Ava thought something was up when she insisted that she would be the one in the courtroom when Susie Mercer took the stand, and Karen didn't argue.

"We're going to need someone who's already familiar with the case," Karen explained. "I assumed you still wanted in. But there's one catch."

"There always is."

"We want you to come work for us."

Ava sat there, mouth open.

"Don't look so surprised, Ava. We've been trying to recruit you since you graduated law school."

"I figured it was just because of my father," she said.

"We've had someone from our law department contacting you every few months. The DEA doesn't often do things like that out of kindness. You're good, Ava. On top of your game. You've got a lot of your dad in you. You'd be perfect here."

"So I'd be a member of the DEA?"

"If you pass the tests," Karen said, smiling. "Even though you'd be working in a different capacity than a field agent, we'd still require you to go through the training."

"Would I still be under protection?"

"In a sense. You'd be bringing down O'Rourke from behind the scenes. Him, and others like him. It might not put you out in the public eye, but you'd be doing what you'd always wanted to do. At least, that's the way Leo sees it."

She'd have the force of the DEA backing her, with top-secret databases and resources at her fingertips.

It would mean helping people on a much different level, and a different kind of help than what she was used to giving as she fought for victims in the courtroom. While the job would be less personal, it would mean doing something good on a much larger scale.

So many exciting things were happening, but she couldn't wrap her mind around any of them. Not until she sorted out Justin, once and for all.

"I can't give you an answer yet," she told Karen. "I have a matter I need to attend to."

"You're a strong woman, Ava. There aren't a lot of men who can handle that." Karen tapped her fingers along the wheel.

"Yes, well, I know someone strong enough. I just have to figure out if I can put my money where my big mouth is," she muttered. But, for the first time since all of this began, she felt that strength return, the kind that got her through law school and beyond, through some of her toughest cases.

The same strength that was going to pull her through this with Justin.

20

LEO PARKED THE CAR just off of the main road and made the rest of the trip on foot.

"It's about a mile off the bend," the man at the gas station had told him. The only cabin that has plants growing in the yard.

Now he stood by the gate and wondered what it was about this woman that had him traveling fourteen-plus hours in hopes of just seeing her again.

He'd broken in to her apartment with more ease than the typical criminal. It was a skill every good agent learned. In order to beat the bad guys, you had to be able to do what they did, and do it better. But he had to figure out where she'd gone.

There wasn't much to help him. By the looks of things, she'd probably lived here a couple of years, but hadn't bothered to personalize much of the place. All the walls were white. Plain white blinds, as well, the ones that came with the rental, accented the windows. The scent of lilac caught his nose. The plants rested on the kitchen windowsill along with a small vase of sad-looking daisies.

There were no personal papers here, although he guessed she was the type to keep all of that locked in a safe-deposit box somewhere.

Her bag with her wallet was also here. Checkbook. Bills. Cell phone. If she'd been back here recently, she'd left again in a hurry.

Would she really just leave all this behind and disappear? He had enough trouble doing that when he went under, and he'd known there was a beginning and an end. She'd been doing this indefinitely.

The night was humid. And as he stood outside what was surely her house, he stuck his hands in his pockets and foolishly felt as if he was back in high school. Why was he more nervous about approaching Callie now than he'd ever been about anyone? He had the urge to grab some of the flowers and present them to her when he knocked on the door.

But that would mean destroying the lilac bushes she'd obviously planted with care. It meant disrupting her life.

Callie was in there, and she most certainly did not want to be found. Especially not by him. Before he lost his nerve, he shoved the envelope that he'd been holding into the mailbox by the side of the door. Then as much as it killed him to do so, he turned tail and walked away from the small house surrounded by lilac bushes.

To THIS DAY, Justin hated to be awakened by a ringing phone. His job necessitated that, but he thought that over time the memory would fade. Yet every single ring jolted him out of sleep and he'd have that same, awful feeling of picking up the phone and receiving that terrible news....

Monday morning. He had been sleeping off the weekend, had planned to skip most of his morning classes. By that point, his parents had pretty much given up on his graduating on time, which he did to spite them. So he yanked the covers up over his head as the light began to stream in through his window.

He barely slept in his room anymore and he'd forgotten how easily the morning light came through if he forgot to close the shades.

Mainly he kept them open because it gave him the feeling of freedom, let him know that he could escape from his big stuffy house. Anytime he wanted to, he could reach out the window to grab the branch of the old oak tree and shimmy down to the ground.

And he'd prepared to drift off into peaceful sleep, but the phone kept ringing and ringing. His phone. The line his parents kept just for him, although he was certain they monitored his conversations, so he barely used it.

"Dammit. What?" he mumbled into the receiver.

"Justin." It was Turk. And the way his friend said his name made Justin's blood run cold. He'd gotten out of bed before he'd realized it, was yanking on clothes and a baseball hat and would have been out the door if Turk hadn't been crying on the other end. So Justin sat there, on his bed, and listened, even as Justin felt his own world begin to crumble.

Turk's father, Steven, had been mentoring Justin for the past year. He hadn't been around all that much, but whenever he was, Justin felt as if he finally had a father who got him, who understood where his passions, his drive, really lay.

Steve had regaled him and Turk with stories from his Delta days and his current job. He'd given both of the boys, who were nearly, but not quite, men yet, some sound advice on getting the kinds of careers they wished for.

He'd spoken to Justin in private about his own failed marriage. Told him how Turk's mother had been pregnant with Turk when they'd married, that maybe, if that hadn't happened, he would've remained single.

"My job's meant for a single man," Steve told him, his

voice quiet and without arrogance. "But I'd always hoped that maybe there was a woman out there willing to deal with it all."

"Justin, are you there?" It was Cash. Justin clutched the phone receiver hard and let the haze clear from his mind. He'd picked up the phone but hadn't said a word into the receiver.

"Yeah, I'm here," he replied.

IT'S FOR the best.

Justin held on to those words as he finished the O-course and let the doc examine him so he could be cleared for the next mission—all SOP.

When Ava's dad had been killed while working under-cover and Turk had finally calmed down enough for Justin to hang up the phone and book him a ticket home, Justin had gone straight to Ava.

He'd promised Turk he'd stay with her until Turk came home from UCal where he was halfway through his first year of college.

Ava had been so strong. She'd held him while he'd cried for her dad. And then she'd made him dinner and made all the plans as he sat there feeling as if his life had bottomed out as much as hers and Turk's had. And finally, he'd refused Turk's room and the couch in favor of the floor by Ava's bed.

Sometime during the night she'd ended up curled next to him on the floor for comfort, and only then, in the dark, had she cried for her father.

Now, after a quick shower and a change of clothes, Justin went into the meeting room and found Rev there already. For an hour, the two men silently worked through a stack of paperwork, until Justin passed Rev a file and said, "It's over. I don't think I want to talk about it."

Rev pushed back in his chair in his usual attempt at balancing on two back legs, always a fifty-fifty proposition and always funny when he tipped over. "I hear you're moving out."

"I'm ready," Justin said, if only to try to convince himself. He'd been training hard for the past forty-eight hours, training that kept him almost too busy to think. He'd just have to go on like that. Take it one day at a time until the dull ache went away completely.

"Yes, I know. We're always ready. So, are you going to call Ava before we go?"

"I thought we weren't going to talk about that."

"I never agreed to that, boo." Rev slipped into his Cajun-speak whenever he was trying to charm someone into doing something they didn't want to do. And Justin definitely did not want to do this.

"I'm going to go out and do what I need to do for the mission tonight," Justin repeated. "I'm going to get on with my life."

"Without even talking to her?"

"We talked, Rev. We talked and talked and we went around in circles." Justin saw Cash standing by the doorway. "Don't you start."

"I didn't say a word. That's your guilty conscience talking," Cash said.

"I don't have a guilty conscience." Cash had moved in closer and Rev didn't say a word. "Ah, fuck you, Cash. How do you know that?"

"I know that because you love her."

"You used to tell me it was lust."

"Well, I know better now," Cash said.

Justin opened his mouth to shoot it off again, to tell Cash and Rev to leave him the hell alone, but he couldn't. Not with the look he saw in Cash's eyes. He'd seen that same look when Cash thought he'd lost his girlfriend, Rina, last year.

Cash got it. Rev did, too. Everyone got it but him.

"Shit."

"You always were the most stubborn of all of us," Cash said, as if that was some kind of compliment.

"I can't believe you just said that," Justin mumbled. "Hunt's way more stubborn than I am."

Hunt's laughter burst into the room. "Yeah, so, even I got over it."

"Yeah, so, I can't. Neither can she," Justin said quietly, and wished he was anywhere but there.

"Leave him alone. He doesn't need to be distracted right now." Hollywood's frame filled the doorway. He was dressed in full battle fatigues and held a file in his hands. "I need to brief you, Justin. Then we're moving out…0400."

It would be just the two of them this trip—Hollywood and Justin, plus some support from a team of Deltas in the area around the Horn of Africa. Mainly recon. Hours and hours of watching and waiting, of practicing the patience Justin had carefully cultivated since he'd enlisted. It was what he did best.

"Let's roll," he told his CO.

CALLIE HAD FOUND the invitation stuck in her mailbox earlier that morning.

Open if you'd like to come see me.

She'd held the white envelope in her hands for a while, sat outside on the porch and realized that there was no way she could resist.

It contained what she assumed to be Leo's address and telephone number.

Your turn, was all it said underneath.

He's got messy handwriting. Bold, strong. He was sure of himself and somehow managed not to be overbearing.

Which was part of the reason why she was at his door that evening, with no idea what to do beyond knocking.

He answered without asking who it was, swung the door wide wearing nothing but a pair of low-slung jeans, and she couldn't tell if he was surprised to see her or not.

"Come in." He stepped aside and let her cross the threshold. She hesitated briefly because she knew that going in would be easy, but getting out…

"Okay." She brushed past him, close enough to smell the soap on his skin, and heat flooded her body, head to toe. She put a hand to her cheek and wondered if it was too late to turn back.

Leo had closed the door, but he didn't move away from it. No, he wasn't going to make it easy. Not any easier than he already had, anyway.

"You're pissed that I left," she started.

"I was worried," he said. "And pissed."

"Okay. Well, I'm all right. So you don't have to worry anymore."

"That's it?"

"What do you want from me, Leo? I told you at the house that there's nothing between us. It was heat-of-the-moment stuff. The danger. All really romantic, sure, but nothing to build on." She was lying through her teeth.

"Do you make a habit of being completely impossible?" he asked as he padded on bare feet toward her. "I'm just wondering, so I can start making plans."

"Plans for what?"

He was right in front of her, and her resolve to steel herself melted when he smiled at her. God, she was easy around him. Easy and free and happy. "Ways to keep you from being impossible."

"That's never going to happen," she said, tried to pretend

his hands weren't trailing lightly down her bare arms. "Your face—it's healing. I can see both your eyes now."

"Changing the subject?" One hand splayed along her lower back, as if to stop her from bolting. The other continued its lazy exploration of her arms, her neck...

"Your side looks better too," she said quickly. The bruise was purple and yellow, but it didn't seem to bother him.

His hand was playing with her hair. She'd shoved it up into a ponytail for the drive, but he was tugging it down so it tumbled over her shoulders, and when he spoke, his voice was ragged. "Just stay, Callie. Just stay, even if it's just for tonight."

Her body had already relented like the traitor it had been the other night. And Leo knew it. "And what happens tomorrow night?"

"I'll ask you to stay again and you'll say okay."

"How can you be so sure?"

"You came back to me, didn't you?" He pulled her close and she didn't protest. "I know how hard that was for you."

"I don't want to know anything about you, Leo."

"Okay."

"I mean it. I don't want to know what your favorite color is..."

"Blue," he whispered, and she squeezed her eyes shut.

"I don't want to know your favorite foods..."

"Beef stew. Homemade manicotti. I hope you can cook."

Dammit. She could. And what was worse, she wanted to, for him. "I know too much—so much."

"Why don't you want to know more?"

"Because I already know that you can keep me safe."

"That's a bad thing?"

"I don't know...I've never really tried it."

"Let's try," he murmured, his lips brushing the spot on her neck he'd discovered, the one that made her moan softly and shiver against him. "The thing is, you might not want to know anything about me, but I want to know all about you." He traced a finger down the front of her T-shirt.

"You already know more than anyone."

"That's not enough," he said, right before he kissed her. A kiss that started out soft and sweet but soon took her breath away as his mouth took hers more deeply. And then her T-shirt was off, over her head and on the floor, and she was against his chest, her soft moans telling him everything he needed to know.

21

Five days later

AVA HAD BEEN ALLOWED to stop at her house that morning to grab what she'd come to call her trial clothes—black skirt, jacket and shoes. All stylish and conservative, and somber enough for the proceedings, because today, more than ever, was about serious business.

Today's proceedings would implicate Robert Mercer and the O'Rourkes. If things went well, there would be warrants for arrests made, both on state and federal levels. Once that happened, the two could fight it out for who got to prosecute. The main thing was that those men would be off the streets and out of business before they could ever hope to grow into a larger crime syndicate, which was where they were headed.

If Susie hadn't shown up today, the abuse charges would have been canceled and in spite of Leo's testimony, the illegal business dealings would have been difficult to prove and the New York D.A. would be back to the drawing board in terms of moving forward to trial.

But Susie had been there, just as she and Ava had planned weeks earlier. The women had hugged one another under the watchful eye of Karen and a few federal marshals.

The woman who'd left Ava and Callie's care three short weeks before appeared to be a changed person. And not just on the outside. Okay, she'd dyed her normally blond hair a rich shade of brown and had it cut short, but there was a glow of freedom to her cheeks that had been missing before. It was as if Susie had tasted happiness and wasn't going back to her old life.

Ava was more than happy to make sure that didn't happen.

Now, with a tug to her jacket's sleeves, she faced Susie, who sat patiently on the witness stand. Robert Mercer had insisted on being at the proceedings, and Ava was impressed at how well Susie was handling that.

There had been no time to truly prepare Susie for the questions, but most times, Ava found that to be for the best. The natural, underlying emotion of Susie's admissions as to what her life had been like since marrying a secret brother of a powerful drug family had the jury—and the judge—riveted. It was the stuff of heartbreaking television drama, made that much more heart-stopping because it was all true. And, with all eyes focused on Susie, Ava kept her questions brief so she could be all but invisible.

Today was not the day for her to shine.

0220 hours

SINCE THIS WAS a co-mission with a group of Deltas, Justin and his CO stayed aboard their ship by day, acting like tourists looking for some good fishing off the coast of the Horn of Africa.

At night, Justin and Hollywood slipped off the boat and did their jobs. Recon this trip involved a lot of time in the deep blue sea. They'd spent the better part of seventy-two hours fighting the night tides to get to the exact spot Justin had pinpointed days earlier on paper.

Now his camo face paint was slightly smeared from the swim but still effective enough. He and Hollywood treaded around the steel platform of the oil rig in order to reach the beach on the left side. Justin had discovered a path three nights earlier that led directly to the compound, which the CIA believed to be a training ground for terrorist operatives.

After several nights of recon, he believed that the CIA was right on target.

Once on the beach, they crawled to wait in the cover of the cove, until the sights and sounds and smells became familiar to them again. As soon as they'd acclimated well enough to know that tonight was business as usual, they'd make their next crucial move.

It was as good as it got—the night was slightly overcast—no stars and barely a moon.

The only thing on his mind was staying undetected and collecting intel. Two things he excelled at. He and Hollywood communed in near silence as they watched the progression of terrorists slip into the camp.

There were usually at least twenty men acting as guards around the perimeter, and about thirty more who showed up for training. Which meant there was a cache of weapons, equipment and plans.

Yeah, this place had to come down.

On his belly, Justin memorized coordinates and weaponry and counted men until the numbers began to match consistently.

He spoke quietly into his mic. "I can get in there for a better count."

A better count meant less risk for the team who would ultimately take down this terrorist training camp.

"Fifteen minutes," Hollywood said. "I'll cover you." Hollywood was the team's best sniper. There was no better man to watch his back in this situation as he commando crawled silently through the brush. He was beyond thinking. He was all training and focus, and nothing else mattered. Not the bugs or the heat or the light rain that fell. No, he was aware of all those things that could alert him to both safety and danger, but they'd all become a part of him that he couldn't separate from.

He'd moved so slowly through the brush that every second seemed like an hour. Still, the time Hollywood had doled out to him was in the forefront of his mind as he maneuvered around the back of the makeshift building they thought was the armory. Justin pushed through the door slowly.

There were enough weapons here for an entire platoon, and then some. Lockers for forty-five men lined one wall. All of them taken.

As carefully as he'd come, he made the long, silent crawl back to where Hollywood waited.

Intel received. Time to go home.

They humped it to the beach and in tandem they slipped beneath the surface of the cool black water to let the current carry them to the waiting ship.

LEO HADN'T BEEN ABLE to sit still through the last half of the grand jury proceedings, although Callie knew he'd done his best to tamp it down. Months of undercover work, of nonstop action and adrenaline proved that he wouldn't be able to ride a desk anytime soon.

Still, he'd calmed somewhat when she'd laid a hand over his, and he'd beamed with pride at the way Ava handled things.

"Grand jury proceedings aren't usually my thing," he told her hours later as he loosened his tie and slid out of his jacket even before they were down the courthouse steps.

"Today went really well," she said. "It was everything Ava had hoped for." They'd waited around to speak with her after the trial but had barely gotten to say congratulations before Karen whisked her away.

She suspected the only reason she wasn't whisked away herself by the DEA was because she had her own personal agent.

"The actual trial doesn't start for a few weeks," he said as they lagged behind some of the crowd to avoid the telltale press cameras. "I'm testifying, which means I need to lay low. I'll be working out of the office back in Virginia. I'll have lots of time on my hands. And you shouldn't be staying here in the city alone."

"You want me to go back home with you."

"I want you to go back home with me," he agreed. "I'll bring you to the city in time for the trial."

She'd already been staying with him for the past week, most of that time absorbing all the things she hadn't wanted to know about him.

The fact that he was a DEA agent. The way he held her at night, not too smothering, just enough to make her feel comfortable and safe.

The picture of him and Ava she'd discovered on his desk three days before they were due to leave for New York…

"Did you know? About me, I mean," she'd asked.

"I put two and two together after a while," he admitted. "She knows you're all right."

"Why didn't you tell me?"

"I wanted you all to myself for a while."

"Ava's brother…I should have known. Both of you are so…stubborn."

"I'm stubborn?" he asked with a laugh. "Okay, sure, if that's the way you want to play it, I'm the stubborn one."

Now, Callie took his hand and let him guide her through the throng along the courthouse steps, appreciating both his masculine strength and his respect for her.

As he turned back to smile at her, with a look in his eyes that said, *I know,* she knew, too, that letting Leo help her take the lead now and again wasn't all bad. Not at all.

He waited, because he knew she got what he was asking. They began walking along the busy Manhattan sidewalk, moving fast since they were caught up in the notorious street traffic.

"I'm going to help Susie," she called to him above the hustle and bustle. "She'll have round-the-clock protection until this is all over, but then what?"

"Yeah, what about after the trial ends?" To bypass the crowds, they'd stopped and taken shelter against a nearby building.

"She wants me to eventually help her acclimate to her new life. And before you tell me, yes, I know even then it still wouldn't be the safest, but I think—"

"I think this means you're sticking around," he said. "I think it means you won't be that far from me."

"No, only a couple of hours on the shuttle."

"And who knows…once Susie's settled, maybe I can persuade you to make a move. I mean, we need social workers where I live, too." He paused. "You know, what you want to do, and what Susie wants to do, isn't going to be easy."

"Susie said if they want to come get her now for all the things she's talked about, that it doesn't matter. That she did what she needed to, and won't live in fear any longer."

"Brave woman," he murmured, tugging Callie in close to him. "I'm surrounded by brave women."

"And you're happy about that."

"Very."

She'd been pulling him closer, too, her fingers locking around his belt loops right in the middle of downtown Manhattan. "Me, too."

And just like that, Callie knew she'd finally found her way home.

22

AVA COULDN'T REMEMBER a time she'd felt more drained after questioning a witness. She'd been in front of a grand jury before, but this questioning was more important than just taking down the O'Rourkes. It was helping her brother, Susie and Callie, and made sure that everything they'd done over the past days and months and years wasn't for nothing. An awesome responsibility, and one she relished.

With Leo and Callie supporting her, Ava got through it. And while she wouldn't be lead counsel, or any counsel at all once the actual trial began, she'd been there in the clutch.

Susie's appearance, along with Leo's testimony, rocked the courthouse. And now, Ava was free. Free to stay in New York and go back to the D.A.'s office or free to go to the DEA.

Free. And still, no word from Justin.

She'd thought about calling him at least once every hour the first few days they'd been apart. She assumed the obsession would wane. But by the time the trial was over and it hadn't, she knew it was time to act. And a phone call wasn't going to cut it.

By ten that morning, she'd gained admittance onto the base thanks to a call from Leo. She drove the rental car behind the military jeep that escorted her to the SEALs area. The marine in the jeep pointed to a building close to the beach and she waved in thanks.

She was out of her car and in that building in record time, without knocking.

"Hey." A man dressed in jungle BDUs came out of nowhere, held out a hand and blocked her path. He wasn't as tall as Justin, but he was pretty big. And good-looking, too. "This is a restricted area."

She fumbled in her bag for the ID they'd given her. "I'm looking for—"

"I don't care who you're looking for. This is a restricted area, ma'am, and you'll have to leave," the man repeated, his tone leaving no room for argument.

Well, no room for most people, anyway. "I'm not leaving," she said.

He tried to brush past her, but she put her hand out and grabbed his arm. His blue eyes flashed and then, just as suddenly as the anger showed, it disappeared.

"Please," she started over. "I'm looking for—"

"Justin."

"Yes. I'm—"

"Ava."

"Are you going to finish all my sentences?"

He stood in front of her as if forming a protective wall between her and his friend.

Which really, she had to admire. "I'm in love with him," she said.

The man drew himself up sharply, stared into her eyes to gauge the truth in her words.

She must've passed the lie detector test because he stuck his hand out. "I'm Cash."

She took his hand in hers. "I've heard a lot about you."

"Ditto."

They smiled at one another. "Are you going to help me find him?"

Cash paused for a second. "I'd like to help you, Ava, but I can't. Justin's not here right now."

She stared into Cash's bluer-than-blue eyes for a second, thinking he was merely trying to put her off again, until her stomach knotted and she finally got what he was telling her. "He's really *not* here."

"Right."

"Has he been gone…long?" she asked.

Cash shifted, looked over his shoulder before answering her. "Not too long. A few weeks."

"Have you heard anything? I mean, does he check in?"

Cash didn't answer.

He can't answer you.

But that logic didn't stop her from feeling dizzy.

"Hey, Ava. Ava?" Cash's voice sounded kind of far away and she heard a rush of other voices around her. In seconds, she was being picked up and carried, then set down somewhere and instructed to put her head between her legs and breathe.

"Bring her some Gatorade or something," she heard someone drawl, a southern accent, but different from Justin's.

"Justin," she whispered just for the hell of it.

"No, sorry, ma'am. I'm Rev."

She looked into the eyes of a dark-haired man who handed her a drink that was blue. She took a few tentative sips while the men around her spoke to one another.

"I don't understand it. One second she was asking about Justin, the next, she was fainting," Cash was saying.

"What did you tell her about Justin?"

"Just that he's not here right now."

"Jesus, Cash, you scared her. She's freaked about us as it is," Rev said.

"About us?" Cash asked.

"Yeah, like what we do for a living. Her dad was Delta. She gets it too much."

The men were all looking at her. She wondered if her tongue was blue, and what they would do if she stuck it out at them.

She didn't bother to find out. "Yes, I get it too much. Your job freaks me out. I already told Justin that. So I just don't get it. I want to know how the women in your lives handle all of this. Because, so far, I'm not doing a very good job of it."

"You're freaked out about our job and want to know how the women in our lives handle it?" Hunt repeated, as if it was the most ridiculous question in the entire world. "How about how we deal with the women in our lives?"

"What is he talking about?" she asked Rev, who just shrugged. "What are you talking about?" she asked Hunt.

"The women in our lives happen to think that living dangerously applies to them. And when we tell them that what they're doing is dangerous and maybe, maybe they could just slow down or look around or listen to us, because we know what we're talking about, do they listen? No!" Hunt looked to Cash for support.

"Seriously. Rina doesn't listen to me when I ask her to maybe rethink where she's shooting her documentary. I mean, freakin' Botswana?" Cash stared at Ava as though she knew how to stop this Rina person.

"Carly wants to surf Pipe again. 'Just for fun,' she says. Yeah, fun."

"Carly's pro-surfing career ended at Pipe," Rev explained. "It was pretty bad, but she seems to be over the fear."

"And then there's you," Hunt said, and he and Cash both stared her down.

"Me?"

"Yes, getting involved in this case the way you did without thinking about your own personal safety," Hunt said.

"And you'd do it again, wouldn't you?" Cash asked before turning to Hunt. "That's what Rina always says. 'I'd do it again, John.' Like calling me by my first name is going to get through to me." Cash snorted.

"Carly was surfing with a broken collarbone last week. Said, 'It's already broken, so what's the harm?'" Hunt shared an exasperated look with her.

She looked at Rev.

"Don't look at me—I'm single," he said.

"The thing is, we encouraged them to do these things, live their dreams. They were all worried about us—the work we do. And now Rina's going back to Botswana," Cash finished, as though that explained everything.

The strange thing was, it did.

"You're a good match for Justin," Rev stage-whispered. "That's what they're telling you, in case you didn't get it."

"I get it, Rev," she said. "For the first time, I get it."

AN HOUR LATER, Ava was standing outside watching the men, Cash, Hunt and Rev, debate each other at the corner of the beach near the parking lot. Rev quit the discussion and offered to drive her car back to where she was staying.

Before she could reply that she hadn't figured that one out yet, the men began to argue again, and a convertible pulled up with surfboards sticking out of the opened rooftop. A tall, blond, athletic-looking woman got out of the car, and Hunt, who'd been yelling the loudest, came right over to her. His-eyes locked on the woman's, who could only be Carly of the broken collarbone, and even Ava's stomach flipped a little because of the way Hunt looked at her.

It was the same way Justin looked at Ava. Demanding, infuriatingly sexy. Loving.

Carly said something to Hunt that made him smile and he pulled her in for a brief kiss.

"That's Hunt's Carly," Rev said.

She hadn't noticed the SEAL had come up beside her. "I kind of figured," she said, then saw Rev was holding a key out to her. "Is that for me?"

"Yes."

"What's it to?"

"Justin's house."

"I can't stay there," she said. "He wouldn't want me there."

"Then he can tell you that himself when he comes back. You don't seem like the kind of woman to change her mind once you've finally made it up."

"You're right, Rev."

"Come on, let me drive you to his house."

"Okay. Hey, look, I know you can't…I mean, I know he's away, but—"

"Ask me no questions and I'll tell you no lies," he said. "Just have some faith. They did."

She watched Hunt climb into the passenger's side of the car and wave to his teammates as Carly drove them away.

Ava had already resigned from the D.A.'s office, was still thinking on the DEA's offer. Plenty of time with nothing to do but think. And invade Justin's home without an invitation.

23

Two weeks later

"Justin's going to hate it," Ava said.

"He'll get used to it. Eventually. If he wears sunglasses all the time when he comes in here," Carly offered. Then the two women took their gazes away from the kitchen wall they'd just painted a far too vibrant pink, and looked at each other and burst out laughing.

"It didn't seem this bright on the paint-color chip," Ava said once she caught her breath.

"It kind of did," Carly replied. "But there was no talking you out of it."

"Yes, well, tell me something I don't know." Ava groaned, and put the paint roller down into its pan.

Carly had been the first one to visit Ava the day after Ava had moved herself into Justin's house with the same, familiar spirit she'd used to throw herself into any new task. She was going to prove to Justin that she could do this, even if it killed her.

Although one look at this wall, and given the way she'd taken over pretty much every available closet in the house, might just have him taking her down first.

Since meeting Carly, and then Cash's girlfriend, Rina, Ava had spent a good deal of time with both women. They talked about everything from their jobs to the SEAL team in general. And their men, with specifics. Carly had also started to teach Ava to surf.

Rina's friend Stella came up for a few nights, too, and suddenly Ava found herself with a newfound appreciation for tarot cards and palm reading thanks to Stella's New Age approach to life.

Stella told her that Ava's aura was very strong, and that if she ever wanted to give up being a lawyer, she had a good future in tarot-card reading.

Beyond Callie, Ava hadn't spent any significant amount of time bonding with other women. Carly and Rina were both so independent. They were really just like Hunt and Cash had described them—stubborn, full of life, risk-takers.

They were awesome women.

"Awesome women deserve awesome men," Carly had commented when Ava complimented her earlier in the week. "I think what you did for your client is pretty awesome, as well."

Yes, Ava had done something good there with Susie. Now it was time to move on to a job so she could help on a larger scale, with the DEA.

Carly rifled through Justin's fridge and came up with two sodas. "We can repaint tomorrow," she offered. "That way Justin won't totally freak out when he gets home."

"I wish I knew when that was," Ava said, and Carly nodded in that join-the-club fashion. Hunt and Cash had both gone wheels up last week themselves, and Ava was more than grateful for the support system. That was one piece of the puzzle that was missing from her parents' marriage—the support system was something her mom never seemed to have.

Ava realized that was something she wouldn't be able to do without, no matter how independent she was.

"You're thinking too much again," Carly called out.

"I know, I know."

"Is your life going to be better with Justin than it would be without him?" Carly asked. "If the answer's yes, then nothing else matters."

"The answer's always been yes," Ava admitted as Carly's phone began to ring.

Carly smiled at Ava as she pulled her cell phone out of her pocket, then glanced at the viewfinder hopefully. "It's Rev," she said, opened the phone and began to speak. "Hey, Rev, what's up?"

Ava had been busy moving away the sheets they'd been using as drop cloths, stopped and turned only when she heard a soft gasp from Carly. The woman, whose complexion was normally a beautiful golden tanned color, had gone ashen, and she clutched the phone to her ear. But it was as if she'd lost the power of speech.

And then she started shaking her head back and forth, a silent no, and that's when Ava took the phone from Carly's hand and put it to her own ear, a hand on Carly's shoulder the entire time.

"Rev, it's Ava. What's going on?" she asked tentatively.

"I'm glad someone's with her. I can't leave base and I didn't want Carly to find out any other way." The drawl wasn't as pronounced because of his clipped tones and she knew immediately that something was wrong. "Hunt's MIA. You need to remain calm. For Carly. I'll be in touch as soon as I have any intel, but don't you dare show that woman fear. You have faith."

"I'll take care of it, Rev."

She clicked the phone closed.

"He's fine, Ava," Carly said immediately, as though she'd been having a mental argument with herself on the subject while Ava had been on the phone. It was as if she'd pulled herself together in mere seconds. But Ava knew from experience that *together* in a situation like this was a relative term. "If Hunt wasn't all right, I would know."

"Of course you would. I believe you." And Ava did, could see the hope shining clear and strong in Carly's eyes.

"I want to go home. Will you drive me there? I want to be there when Hunt calls. I need to be near his things."

Ava didn't wait for her to finish, was nodding, guiding the tall blonde out to her car, taking her back to the small house about a half hour away from Justin's, on the opposite side of the base.

Carly and Hunt had just moved into the house a few months earlier. Carly had sold her place in Florida, had other people managing her surfing business so she could be closer to Hunt.

"I gave up bigger waves, but he's worth it," Carly had told her earlier that week when they were at the beach. "Hunt might get transferred to a team in Hawaii…that would be cool for both of us."

The second they got into the house, Carly changed out of her tank top into a T-shirt of Hunt's. "It's my favorite," she explained. "It still smells like him."

Ava stopped Carly to give her a hug as she suddenly had an urge to go grab one of Justin's T-shirts and do the same thing.

"GOOD TO BE HOME," Hollywood yelled. He stretched his legs in the Blackhawk that was bringing him and Justin back to base.

Home. Justin hadn't allowed himself to think about it beyond that one little word, about what he would be, and wouldn't be, coming home to. So he nodded to his CO and he smiled and then he put his head back and let himself process how many days he'd been gone, how much time had passed.

Where Ava would be right now.

Done with the grand jury hearing. Back at work at the D.A.'s office. Getting ready for the trial.

Not anywhere in his vicinity.

"You're thinking about a woman," Hollywood called.

"Maybe."

"Only women can make you frown like that."

"Yeah, that's true."

"You did good out there. You kept your private life out of it. Stayed focused," Hollywood continued, and Justin wondered what the hell he was trying to say. "You're ready, Brandt. Ready for anything."

His CO gave him a thumbs-up before turning his attention to other things. Justin considered whether Hollywood had been hanging around with his tarot-card-reading sometime-girlfriend for too long.

He wanted to tell Hollywood that he wasn't the problem, that he'd always been ready. Instead, he closed his eyes and let the movement of the helo distract him until they landed.

24

JUSTIN WAS HOME. She'd heard his bike pull up and then his key was in the lock within seconds and his gun was pulled, because he'd seen the lights on all over the house.

"It's me, Justin. It's Ava," she called before she came into his sight. He was already lowering his gun.

"How did you get in here?" was the first thing he asked, followed quickly by, "Why is one kitchen wall pink?"

"Rev gave me a key," she said, as if that would explain everything from her presence to the paint color.

"Rev gave you a key," he repeated as he walked toward where she stood in the living room.

She'd only come home from Carly's a few hours earlier because Rev told her Justin would be home that evening. The relief that came from hearing those words had been enough to make her tear up.

Rina and Rev assured her that they'd take care of Carly, and Ava promised her that she'd be back soon, with Justin.

Now she saw Justin note the tarot cards and the piles of papers on the coffee table. "Rev told me you were on your way home. But he said you had to stop at the hospital. Are you all right?" she asked.

This was the first time she'd ever seen him dressed in his SEAL gear. Camouflage-patterned pants and heavy boots, a black T-shirt stretching across his chest, and he still had fine traces of paint on his face. It was amazing and heartbreaking all at the same time.

"I'm all right," he said finally, but she didn't believe him. Not totally, because she knew that even if there was nothing wrong with him physically, he still knew about Hunt.

She walked over to where he stood and began checking him for bandages and bullet holes just in case, and she thought she heard him chuckle. "I was at the hospital with my CO. Post-mission physical. He's fine. I'm fine. Everyone's fine."

"Justin…"

He spoke quickly, as if tearing off a Band-Aid. "Hunt's MIA."

"I know about Hunt."

He dropped his bag to the ground and nodded. "I was going to change before I went to see Carly. I figured going like this might…" He trailed off absently as he started to peel off his T-shirt.

"Yes, that's a good idea." She touched his shoulder gently. "Go change and then we'll drive over to Carly's. I told her I'd be back soon."

He stared at her. "You were with her today?"

"I was there when she got the call. I stayed until Rina and Rev got there. Rev said you were on your way home and I wanted to be here."

Justin looked as if he wanted to say something to her, but he merely nodded instead and began shrugging out of his clothes as he headed toward the bedroom.

"You've got to be the calm one," Rina told her just the other day. "Being calm helps them. They like to see that you're holding it together. That helps them hold it together during times like this. If they fall apart, then you stay strong and you let them."

She could do that now, be strong for Justin. He had his mind filled with worry, for Hunt. For Cash, who was part of the team looking for Hunt.

As the water rained down hard on his back, Justin tried to deal with his conflicting emotions.

Hunt MIA.

Ava here, in his house.

Pink walls.

Hunt MIA. Ava with Carly.

MIA was Ava's worst fear. Any of their worst fears, actually. And yet, she was still here, waiting patiently for him in the kitchen, handing him a soda and a sandwich she'd produced from his suddenly well-stocked refrigerator, and he hadn't even realized he was hungry until he'd spotted the food.

"You don't have to go back there with me," he said after he'd eaten half the sandwich.

"I know. I want to."

"I don't even know what you're doing here."

"We can talk about that later. Let's go to Carly now," she said, tugging him out the door.

He didn't tell her that Hollywood had needed to hold him back from jumping onto the helo they'd just come out of to stop him heading off to find Hunt himself. Actually, Hollywood looked grateful that he had to concentrate on grabbing Justin, because Justin knew his CO was fighting his own urge to do the same.

"We don't have clearance," Hollywood told him. "There's another team inserted. Cash is there. They'll find him."

They'll find him. He had to believe that. But, do nothing wasn't a role he did well.

He hadn't realized that he'd slid into the passenger seat, but he had, so her let Ava drive him to Hunt's place, let her push in one of his favorite CDs for the short trip.

Let her take care of him. And he liked it. A lot. Too much.

Her hand was reaching out for his. They'd parked in front of the house and he'd been staring into space.

Get it together, Brandt.

"I'll help you keep it together," she said, as if she'd read his mind. And then she leaned over and she kissed him, first on the cheek and then on the mouth, a soft, lingering kiss. "I didn't get a chance to hug you. To tell you that I'm so glad you're home."

He wanted to tell her that he was glad, too. That seeing her in his house was the best thing possible, especially considering the news he'd gotten once the helo had landed. But now wasn't the time. "Thanks for coming here with me," he said instead, and she nodded and together they got out of the car and headed up the driveway.

Rev was still there with Rina. Hollywood was there, too, and a few other guys from the team, as well. Ava went immediately to Carly while Rev came over to Justin.

"No word on anything yet," Rev told him.

"Cash hasn't checked in?"

Rev shot him a quick look. "They can't get him on radio at all anymore."

Shit. *Shit.*

"You should go home—you just got back—you're exhausted," Rev said.

"I need to be here for Carly."

"You're going to make things worse unless you get that look off your face," Rev told him urgently, but it was too late. Carly was already moving toward him, was hugging him fiercely. And somehow, again, a woman was the one comforting him when he was supposed to be the strong one.

"He's fine, Justin. He and Cash both," Carly whispered in his ear.

"Of course they are."

"Have you eaten?" Carly asked.

"You don't have to worry about me."

"Sure I do. That's the job of a wife of a SEAL—I get to worry about all of you." There was no sarcasm in her tone at all, no resentment, just pure faith.

He looked across the room where Ava stood with Rina and Hollywood.

"Ava's cool," Carly said. "And don't worry, we're going to repaint the pink wall."

He smiled in spite of himself.

"I called Ty, told him to stay in Florida for now," Carly continued, referencing Hunt's brother.

"Did he listen?"

"I'm expecting to hear his Harley coming up the block any time now."

"Well, it'll give him something to do," Justin said. "He'd go crazy sitting at home waiting. I know he and Samantha want to be here for you."

"And Hunt's going to have a fit and tell all of you that you made too big a deal over nothing," Carly added, and yes, that would be something that Hunt would do. That was exactly what they all wanted Hunt to do.

"Carly, your mom's on the phone," Rina called out. Carly went to answer it. Justin drew in a deep breath and looked at his team members and at the wives and girlfriends and at Ava and remembered all the times he wished that Ava had been there, with him and his friends.

That's when the room grew far too small for him and he headed for air.

TEN MINUTES LATER, Ava found him on Carly and Hunt's back deck, staring up into the sky, where he'd been trying to relay messages to Cash and Hunt through telepathy, mainly of the will-you-fucking-call-in-now variety. She didn't say a word, didn't try to analyze him, just put her hand on his shoulder and stared up into the sky the same way he was doing.

They stayed like that for what could've been hours or minutes—he lost track.

"How are you staying so calm?" he finally asked her.

"I don't have a choice." She reached for his hand, held it tight. "I know what you're thinking. That I'm going to get through this and then I'm going to freak out about everything that's happened."

Yeah, those had pretty much been his thoughts. Ava was excellent under pressure, but once she was given time to sit back and digest the things that happened under that pressure, well, the results wouldn't be pretty. "It could be me, you know. Me you're waiting to hear news on."

"I know that," she said quietly. "But I'm here. You're here. And I'm done spending time worrying about things that might happen. I'm only dealing with things that are in the here and now."

He opened his mouth to answer her, had no idea what he was going to say, when the door behind them slid open with a slam.

It was Rev. "They're on their way home. Mission accomplished."

"Hunt?"

"Broken arm. And Cash is pissed at Hollywood for authorizing marines to come in and look for them. Apparently, Cash had already gotten to Hunt earlier in the day—they just lost comms. Just a giant miscommunication."

From inside the house he heard talking and crying, saw

tears running down Ava's cheeks despite her smile. And he took her into his arms and just held her on the porch until he'd calmed down enough to breathe normally again.

25

JUSTIN DROVE HIMSELF and Ava back to the house after another couple of hours had passed. Even as the skies were breaking open with major spring thunderstorms, the tension in Carly's house had lifted, food had been ordered and Justin's entire body was weak from relief.

When he got back inside his house, with Ava, the tension began to creep in again. And he didn't even know where to begin. All he wanted to do was crawl into bed with Ava and not think about anything else.

But if he didn't get this sorted out now, he was never going to get any relief at all. "You did really great tonight—with Carly," he started as Ava kicked her wet shoes off and pulled her hair out of the ponytail so it tumbled over her shoulders.

"Only with Carly?"

He sighed. "That's not what I meant. Look, like I said earlier, I don't even know why you're really here. All I know is that you've moved into my house while I was gone and I'm not sure how real any of this is."

"When you saved me—back at the hotel with Agent Harris—you didn't give me a chance to explain."

"I didn't need to wait around for the inevitable. Can we please not go over this again? It nearly killed me the first time."

"You know I love you."

"You've said yourself that you don't want this kind of life."

"I didn't."

"And I'm supposed to believe now that you do?"

"Now I believe that if I want to be with you, I might have to concede a few things."

He stared at her. "Will the real Ava Turkowski please stand up?"

"The DEA's offered me a position in their legal department. I wouldn't be trying cases—my name and face would be kept out of the public eye—but I'd get to work on them, ones like O'Rourke's. From behind the scenes," she said. "For me, it was never about being in the spotlight. It was about doing the right thing."

"Yeah, well, I always knew that."

"I know you did. You've always known me better than anyone else. The same way I know you better than anyone."

"Ava, what are you doing?"

She shrugged. "I guess I'm saving you."

Dammit. That was exactly what she'd done tonight. "So, you'll be working for the DEA?" he asked in an attempt to shift the subject.

"In the office," she amended. "It's not like I'll be out in the field."

He started muttering to himself, and looked around at the stuff she'd brought into his kitchen, into his life, and clenched his fists. "Is that a surfboard by the fridge?"

"Yes—it's mine."

"Since when do you surf?"

"Since Carly taught me. It's very Zenlike. Did you know that there are a lot of women on base who need low-cost legal advice?" she asked.

"How long have you been here?" he asked.

She glanced toward the stuff that had piled up in his absence. "I'm sorry, Justin. I can move all of it…"

"No, don't bother," he said. "It's just that…it kind of looks like a home in here. At last."

He almost relented. Almost. The way Ava gazed at him, her green eyes clear and calm, infuriatingly so, as if she knew she'd won the battle and complete victory couldn't be far behind. But he wasn't that easy of a sell.

"You're not totally safe that way, with the DEA," he told her.

"Neither are you."

"Ava…look, I get it. I love it that you're trying this, meeting with the other guys' wives and girlfriends, trying to get a feeling for all this. But you already know what it's like. You've lived through more nights like tonight with your dad than you want to remember."

"I'd forgotten how much good times there are, too. I'd forgotten about the good things, Justin. I'm not going to do that again."

"It's just because this is all new."

"That's not why and you know it."

"I don't know anything anymore!" he roared. He kicked the table and then each chair and felt only marginally better. He walked outside, into the pouring rain and stood there. He let it wash over him, drench him. Calm him.

He was still fighting but he didn't know what he was fighting anymore. Or why. And when Ava's arms came around his chest from behind he knew that fighting was no longer the answer.

Believing was. And he did believe that Ava loved him. Knew it deep in his heart. Always had.

He turned around to face her. The rain was coming down harder by the second and they were both soaked to the skin.

"I didn't want you to feel trapped," she said. "That's all. I wanted you to be free to make your own choice."

"If I asked you to marry me, would you? Would you have done it back then, if the thing with Gina had never happened? Better yet, would you do it now?" he asked, and then he traced her bottom lip with his thumb. She looked so serious, so beautiful. "I don't expect—don't want your answer now. I just want you to think about it. About the future. About us."

"I think I can do that."

"Good."

"I mean, I think I could marry you."

He forced a smile. "Ava, when I marry you—and I will marry you—make no mistake about that, you won't need to think at all. You'll feel it. It might take another nine years before everything aligns in the right way for us, but I have no doubt it will."

"Justin—"

"I leave again. Day after tomorrow."

"Oh," she said. "Oh."

A long silence stretched between them.

"So, do you want to marry me before you go, or wait until you get back?" she asked matter-of-factly, and he couldn't suppress his laugh. Ava had never failed to surprise him and that was exactly the way he liked it.

"I want to marry you before I go."

"Then let's make it happen. We can find a justice of the peace and wake him or her up."

"Why don't we let him or her sleep and we get married first thing in the morning? Because there's something I need to do first." He scooped her into his arms and walked inside, down the small hallway to the bedroom.

He didn't stop until he'd put her on the bed and she was

helping him strip his wet clothes off while he did the same for her. They were both slippery, slick skin on skin and yes, there was no reason to fight.

His mouth came down on hers, a hard claim. She responded in kind, pressed her body to his so tightly, as if she was never going to let go.

He pulled away from her in order to put his mouth to work in other places. Ones he'd been dreaming about during the free time he'd had over the last three weeks when he wasn't viciously pushing thoughts of her from his head so that he'd be able to do his job.

He kissed up and down her body. Twice. Spent time worshipping her breasts and between her thighs and every other place while she called his name in that breathy voice he loved.

And when he rocked inside of her, he was calling out her name and knew there was no place he'd rather be.

"Did you miss me?" he murmured against her ear once he'd recovered.

"Yes. But you were there the whole time," she whispered. "I dreamed about you every single night. Woke up hugging my pillow."

"I will always be with you. I am—I am always with you."

"As I am with you, Justin."

He stroked her hair tenderly. "I love you, Ava. Always have…"

"Always will," she finished for him. *"Always."*

* * * * *

Enjoy a sneak preview of
MATCHMAKING WITH A MISSION
by B.J. Daniels,
part of the **WHITEHORSE, MONTANA** *miniseries.*
Available from Harlequin Intrigue
in April 2008.

Nate Dempsey has returned to Whitehorse to uncover the truth about his past…

Nate sensed someone watching the house and looked out in surprise to see a woman astride a paint horse just on the other side of the fence. He quickly stepped back from the filthy second-floor window, although he doubted she could have seen him. Only a little of the June sun pierced the dirty glass to glow on the dust-coated floor at his feet as he waited a few heartbeats before he looked out again.

The place was so isolated he hadn't expected to see another soul. Like the front yard, the dirt road was waist-high with weeds. When he'd broken the lock on the back door, he'd had to kick aside a pile of rotten leaves that had blown in from last fall.

As he sneaked a look, he saw that she was still there, staring at the house in a way that unnerved him. He shielded his eyes from the glare of the sun off the dirty window and studied her, taking in her head of long blond hair that feathered out in the breeze from under her Western straw hat.

She wore a tan canvas jacket, jeans and boots. But it was the way she sat astride the brown-and-white horse that nudged the memory.

He felt a chill as he realized he'd seen her before. In that very spot. She'd been just a kid then. A kid on a pretty paint horse. Not this one—the markings were different. Anyway, it couldn't have been the same horse, considering the last time he had seen her was more than twenty years ago. That horse would be dead by now.

His mind argued it probably wasn't even the same girl. But he knew better. It was the way she sat the horse, so at home in a saddle and secure in her world on the other side of that fence.

To the boy he'd been, she and her horse had represented freedom, a freedom he'd known he would never have—even after he escaped this house.

Nate saw her shift in the saddle, and for a moment he feared she planned to dismount and come toward the house. With Ellis Harper in his grave, there would be little to keep her away.

To his relief, she reined her horse around and rode back the way she'd come.

As he watched her ride away, he thought about the way she'd stared at the house—today and years ago. While the smartest thing she could do was to stay clear of this house, he had a feeling she'd be back.

Finding out her name should prove easy, since he figured she must live close by. As for her interest in Harper House... He would just have to make sure it didn't become a problem.

* * * * *

Be sure to look for
MATCHMAKING WITH A MISSION
and other suspenseful Harlequin Intrigue stories,
available in April
wherever books are sold.

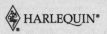

HARLEQUIN®

INTRIGUE®

⧫ WHITEHORSE ⧫
MONTANA

No matter how much Nate Dempsey's past haunted
him, McKenna Bailey couldn't keep him off her mind.
He'd returned to town to bury his troubled youth—
but she wouldn't stop pursuing him until he was
working on the ranch by her side.

Look for

MATCHMAKING
WITH A
MISSION

BY

B.J. DANIELS

Available in April
wherever books are sold.

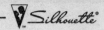

SPECIAL EDITION™

Introducing a brand-new miniseries

Men of
Mercy Medical

Gabe Thorne moved to Las Vegas to open a
new branch of his booming construction
business—and escape from a recent tragedy.
But when his teenage sister showed up pregnant
on his doorstep, he really had his hands full.
Luckily, in turning to Dr. Rebecca Hamilton for
the medical care his sister needed, he found
a cure for himself....

Starting with

THE MILLIONAIRE
AND THE M.D.
by *TERESA SOUTHWICK,*

available in April wherever books are sold.

nocturne™

The Bloodrunners
trilogy continues with book #2.

The hunt meant more to Jeremy Burns than dominance—
it meant facing the woman he left behind. Once
Jillian Murphy had belonged to Jeremy, but now she was
the Spirit Walker to the Silvercrest wolves. It would take
more than the rights of nature for Jeremy to renew his
claim on her—and she would not go easily once he had.

LAST WOLF
HUNTING

by RHYANNON BYRD

Available in April wherever books are sold.

Be sure to watch out for the last book,
Last Wolf Watching, available in May.

SN61785

*Things are heating up
aboard Alexandra's Dream....*

Coming in March 2008

ISLAND
HEAT

by

Sarah Mayberry

It's been eight years since Tory Sanderson found
out that Ben Cooper seduced her to win a bet...
and eight years since she got her revenge. Now
aboard *Alexandra's Dream* as a guest lecturer for
her cookbook, she is shocked to discover the
guest chef joining her is none other than Ben!
And when these two ex-lovers reunite, the heat
starts to climb...in and out of the kitchen!

*Available in March 2008
wherever books are sold.*

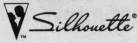

Romantic
SUSPENSE

**Sparked by Danger,
Fueled by Passion.**

The Taken

Tierney Doyle is used to being criticized for
her psychic abilities, yet the tough-as-nails—
and drop-dead-gorgeous—detective has no doubt
about what she has uncovered in the case of a
string of unsolved murders. And Tierney is slowly
discovering that working so close to her partner,
detective Wade Callahan, could be lethal.

Look for

Danger Signals
by Kathleen Creighton

Available in April wherever books are sold.

REQUEST YOUR FREE BOOKS!

2 FREE NOVELS PLUS 2 FREE GIFTS!

HARLEQUIN®

Blaze™

Red-hot reads!

YES! Please send me 2 FREE Harlequin® Blaze™ novels and my 2 FREE gifts (gifts are worth about $10). After receiving them, if I don't wish to receive any more books, I can return the shipping statement marked "cancel". If I don't cancel, I will receive 6 brand-new novels every month and be billed just $4.24 per book in the U.S. or $4.71 per book in Canada, plus 25¢ shipping and handling per book and applicable taxes, if any*. That's a savings of 15% or more off the cover price! I understand that accepting the 2 free books and gifts places me under no obligation to buy anything. I can always return a shipment and cancel at any time. Even if I never buy another book, the two free books and gifts are mine to keep forever.

151 HDN ERVA   351 HDN ERUX

Name	(PLEASE PRINT)	
Address		Apt. #
City	State/Prov.	Zip/Postal Code

Signature (if under 18, a parent or guardian must sign)

Mail to the **Harlequin Reader Service**:
IN U.S.A.: P.O. Box 1867, Buffalo, NY 14240-1867
IN CANADA: P.O. Box 609, Fort Erie, Ontario L2A 5X3

Not valid to current subscribers of Harlequin Blaze books.

Want to try two free books from another line?
Call 1-800-873-8635 or visit www.morefreebooks.com.

* Terms and prices subject to change without notice. N.Y. residents add applicable sales tax. Canadian residents will be charged applicable provincial taxes and GST. This offer is limited to one order per household. All orders subject to approval. Credit or debit balances in a customer's account(s) may be offset by any other outstanding balance owed by or to the customer. Please allow 4 to 6 weeks for delivery. Offer available while quantities last.

Your Privacy: Harlequin Books is committed to protecting your privacy. Our Privacy Policy is available online at www.eHarlequin.com or upon request from the Reader Service. From time to time we make our lists of customers available to reputable third parties who may have a product or service of interest to you. If you would prefer we not share your name and address, please check here. ☐

HB08

HARLEQUIN®

Blaze™

COMING NEXT MONTH